The Cay

with
Connections

The Cay

Theodore Taylor

with
Connections

HOLT, RINEHART AND **WINSTON**
Harcourt Brace & Company

Austin • New York • Orlando • Atlanta • San Francisco
Boston • Dallas • Toronto • London

For permission to reprint copyrighted material, grateful acknowledgment is made to the following sources:

Bantam Doubleday Dell Books for Young Readers, a division of Bantam Doubleday Dell Publishing Group, Inc., New York, New York: *The Cay* by Theodore Taylor. Copyright © 1969 by Theodore Taylor. All rights reserved.

Arte Público Press: From "One More Lesson" from *Silent Dancing: A Partial Remembrance of a Puerto Rican Childhood* by Judith Ortiz Cofer. Copyright © 1990 by Judith Ortiz Cofer. Published by Arte Público Press-University of Houston, 1990. **HarperCollins Publishers:** Excerpt (retitled "Lost on the Tundra") from "Amaroq, the wolf" from *Julie of the Wolves* by Jean Craighead George. Copyright © 1972 by Jean Craighead George. **Houghton Mifflin Company:** "The Shark" from *Fast and Slow* by John Ciardi. Copyright © 1975 by John Ciardi. All rights reserved. **Dr. Joseph MacInnis:** "Barracuda" from *Underwater Images* by Joseph MacInnis. Copyright © 1971 by Joseph MacInnis. **Morrow Junior Books, a division of William Morrow & Company, Inc.:** Excerpt (retitled "Without Him We're Dead Meat") from *Far North* by Will Hobbs. Copyright © 1996 by Will Hobbs. **Random House, Inc.:** "The Clever Gander" from *Tales from India,* retold by Asha Upadhyay. Copyright © 1971 by Asha Upadhyay.

Cover illustration by Alan Douglas Dingman

HRW is a registered trademark licensed to Holt, Rinehart and Winston.

Printed in the United States of America

ISBN 0-03-054604-4

21 22 1083 12 11 10
4500251103

To Dr. King's dream,
which can only come true
if the very young know and understand.

LAGUNA BEACH, CALIFORNIA

Contents

CHAPTER

One

LIKE SILENT, HUNGRY SHARKS that swim in the darkness of the sea, the German submarines arrived in the middle of the night.

I was asleep on the second floor of our narrow, gabled green house in Willemstad, on the island of Curaçao, the largest of the Dutch islands just off the coast of Venezuela. I remember that on that moonless night in February 1942, they attacked the big Lago oil refinery on Aruba, the sister island west of us. Then they blew up six of our small lake tankers, the tubby ones that still bring crude oil from Lake Maracaibo to the refinery, Curaçaosche Petroleum Maatschappij, to be made into gasoline, kerosene, and diesel oil. One German sub was even sighted off Willemstad at dawn.

So when I woke up there was much excitement in the city, which looks like a part of old Holland, except that all the houses are painted in soft colors, pinks and greens and blues, and there are no dikes.

It was very hard to finish my breakfast because I wanted to go to Punda, the business district, the oldest part of town, and then to Fort Amsterdam where I could look out to sea. If there was an enemy U-boat out there, I wanted to see it and join the people in shaking a fist at it.

I was not frightened, just terribly excited. War was something I'd heard a lot about, but had never seen. The whole world was at war, and now it had come to us in the warm, blue Caribbean.

The first thing that my mother said was, "Phillip, the enemy has finally attacked the island, and there will be no school today. But you must stay near home. Do you understand?"

I nodded, but I couldn't imagine that a shell from an enemy submarine would pick me out from all the buildings, or hit me if I was standing on the famous pontoon bridge or among the ships way back in the Schottegat or along St. Anna Bay.

So later in the morning, when she was busy making sure that all our blackout curtains were in place,

and filling extra pots with fresh water, and checking
our food supply, I stole away down to the old
fort with Henrik van Boven, my Dutch friend who
was also eleven.

I had played there many times with Henrik and
other boys when we were a few years younger,
imagining we were defending Willemstad against
pirates or even the British. They once stormed the
island, I knew, long ago. Or sometimes we'd pretend we were the Dutch going out on raids against
Spanish galleons. That had happened too. It was
all so real that sometimes we could see the tall
masted ships coming over the horizon.

Of course, they were only the tattered-sailed native schooners from Venezuela, Aruba, or Bonaire
coming in with bananas, oranges, papayas, melons,
and vegetables. But to us, they were always pirates,
and we'd shout to the noisy black men aboard
them. They'd laugh back and go, "Pow, pow, pow!"

The fort looks as though it came out of a storybook, with gun ports along the high wall that faces
the sea. For years, it guarded Willemstad. But this
one morning, it did not look like a storybook fort
at all. There were real soldiers with rifles and we
saw machine guns. Men with binoculars had them
trained toward the whitecaps, and everyone was
tense. They chased us away, telling us to go home.

Instead, we went down to the Koningin Emma
Brug, the famous Queen Emma pontoon bridge,
which spans the channel that leads to the huge

harbor, the Schottegat. The bridge is built on floats
so that it can swing open as ships pass in or out, and
it connects Punda with Otrabanda, which means
"other side," the other part of the city.

The view from there wasn't as good as from the
fort, but curious people were there, too, just looking. Strangely, no ships were moving in the channel.
The *veerboots*, the ferry boats that shuttled cars
and people back and forth when the bridge was
swung open, were tied up and empty. Even the
native schooners were quiet against the docks inside
the channel. And the black men were not laughing
and shouting the way they usually did.

Henrik said, "My father told me there is nothing
left of Aruba. They hit Sint Nicolaas, you know."

"Every lake tanker was sunk," I said.

I didn't know if that were true or not, but Henrik
had an irritating way of sounding official since his
father was connected with the government.

His face was round and he was chubby. His
hair was straw-colored and his cheeks were always
red. Henrik was very serious about everything he
said or did. He looked toward Fort Amsterdam.

He said, "I bet they put big guns up there now."

That was a safe bet.

And I said, "It won't be long until the Navy is
here."

Henrik looked at me. "Our Navy?" He meant the
Netherlands Navy.

"No," I said. "Ours." Meaning the American Navy,

of course. His little Navy was scattered all over after the Germans took Holland.

Henrik said quietly, "Our Navy will come too," and I didn't want to argue with him. Everyone felt bad that Holland had been conquered by the Nazis.

Then an army officer climbed out of a truck and told us all to leave the Queen Emma bridge. He was very stern. He growled, "Don't you know they could shoot a torpedo up here and kill you all?"

I looked out toward the sea again. It was blue and peaceful, and a good breeze churned it up, making lines of whitecaps. White clouds drifted slowly over it. But I couldn't see the usual parade of ships coming toward the harbor; the stubby ones or the massive ones with flags of many nations that steamed slowly up the bay to the Schottegat to load gas and oil.

The sea was empty; there was not even a sail on it. We suddenly became frightened and ran home to the Scharloo section where we lived.

I guess my face was pale when I went into the house because my mother, who was in the kitchen, asked immediately, "Where have you been?"

"Punda," I admitted. "I went with Henrik."

My mother got very upset. She grabbed my shoulder and shook it. "I told you not to go there, Phillip," she said angrily. "We are at war! Don't you understand?"

"We just wanted to see the submarines," I said.

My mother closed her eyes and pulled me up against her thin body. She was like that. One minute, shaking me; the next, holding me.

The radio was on, and a voice said that fifty-six men had died on the lake tankers that were blown up and that the governor of the Netherlands' West Indies had appealed to Washington for help. There was no use in asking Amsterdam. I listened to the sorrowful sound of his voice until my mother's hand switched it to off.

Finally she said, "You'll be safe if you do what we tell you to do. Don't leave the yard again today."

She seemed very nervous. But then she was often nervous. My mother was always afraid I'd fall off the sea wall, or tumble out of a tree, or cut myself with a pocketknife. Henrik's mother wasn't that way. She laughed a lot and said, "Boys, boys, boys."

Late in the afternoon, my father, whose name was also Phillip—Phillip Enright—returned home from the refinery where he was working on the program to increase production of aviation gas. He'd been up since two o'clock, my mother said, and please don't ask him too many questions.

They had phoned him that morning to say that the Germans might attempt to shell the refinery and the oil storage tanks, and that he must report to help fight the fires. I had never seen him so tired, and I didn't ask as many questions as I wanted to.

Until the past year, my father and I had done a lot of things together. Fishing or sailing our small boat, or taking long hikes around Krup Bay or Seroe Male, or just going out into the *koenoekoe*, the countryside, together. He knew a lot about trees and fish and birds. But now he always seemed busy. Even on a Sunday, he'd shake his head and say, "I'm sorry, guy, I have to work."

After he had had his pint of cold Dutch ale (he had one every night in the living room after he came home), I asked, "Will they shoot at us tonight?"

He looked at me gravely and answered, "I don't know, Phillip. They might. I want you and your mother to sleep down here tonight, not on the second floor. I don't think you're in any danger, but it's better to sleep down here."

"How many of them are out there?" I thought they might be like schools of fish. Dozens, maybe. I wanted to be able to tell Henrik exactly what my father knew about the submarines.

He shook his head. "No one knows, Phillip. But there must be three of them around the islands. The attacks were in three different places."

"They came all the way from Germany?"

He nodded. "Or from bases in France," he said, loading his pipe.

"Why can't we go out and fight them?" I asked.

My father laughed sadly and tapped his long forefinger on my chest. "You'd like that, would you? But we have nothing to fight them with, son. We can't go out in motorboats and attack them with rifles."

My mother came in from the kitchen to say, "Stop asking so many silly questions, Phillip. I told you not to do that."

Father looked at her strangely. He had always answered my questions. "He has a right to know. He's involved here, Grace."

My mother looked back at him. "Yes, unfortunately," she said.

My mother, I knew, had not wanted to come to Curaçao in late 1939, but my father had argued that he was needed for the war effort even though the United States was not at war then. Royal Dutch Shell had borrowed him from his American company because he was an expert in refineries and gasoline production. But the moment she saw it, my mother decided she didn't like Curaçao and she often complained about the smell of gas and oil whenever the trade winds died down.

It was very different in Virginia where my father had been in charge of building a new refinery on the banks of the Elizabeth River. We'd lived in a small white house on an acre of land with many trees. My mother often talked about the house and the trees; about the change of seasons and the friends she had there. She said it was nice and safe in Virginia.

My father would answer quietly, "There's no place nice and safe right now."

I remembered the summers with lightning bugs and honeysuckle smells; the cold winters when the fields would all be brown and would crackle under my feet. I didn't remember too much else. I was only seven when we'd moved to the Caribbean.

I guess my mother was homesick for Virginia, where no one talked Dutch, and there was no smell of gas or oil, and there weren't as many black people around.

Now, there was a cold silence between my mother and my father. Lately, it had been happening more and more often. She went back into the kitchen.

I said to him, "Why can't they use aircraft and bomb the submarines?"

He was staring toward the kitchen and didn't hear me. I repeated it.

He sighed. "Oh yes. Same answer, Phillip. There are no fighting aircraft down here. To tell you the truth, we don't have any weapons."

CHAPTER

TWO

WE FINISHED DINNER just as it was getting dark, and my father went outside to look at our house. He wanted to see if the blackout curtains were working. While my mother and I stood by each window, he called out if he saw the slightest crack of light. By the governor's orders, not a light could shine anywhere on the whole island, he said. Then he went back to the refinery.

I crawled onto the couch downstairs about nine o'clock but I couldn't sleep. I kept thinking about the

U-boats off our coast and those lake tankers with barefooted Chinese sailors on board. I guess I was waiting for the U-boats to send a shell toward Willemstad.

Then I began to wonder if the Germans would send soldiers too. About nine-thirty I sneaked out of bed, went to the tool house, and took a hatchet out. I put it under the couch. It was the only thing I could think of to use for fighting the Germans.

It must have been eleven o'clock when my father returned from the refinery to get all the flashlights we had in the house. They talked in low voices, but I could hear them.

Mother said, "It's too dangerous to stay here now."

My father answered, "Grace, you know I can't leave."

She said, "Well, then Phillip and I must go back. We'll go back to Norfolk and wait until the danger is over."

I sat up in bed, unable to believe what I was hearing. My father said, "There's more danger in the trip back, unless you go by air, than there is in staying here. If they do shell us, they won't hit Scharloo."

Mother said sharply, "You know I won't fly. I'd be frightened to death to fly."

"We'll talk about it later." My father sounded

miserable. Soon afterward he returned to the refinery again.

I thought about leaving the island, and it sad-
dened me. I loved the old fort, and the schooners,
the Ruyterkade market with the noisy chickens and
squealing pigs, the black people shouting; I loved
the koenoekoe with its giant cactus; the divi-divi
trees, their odd branches all on the leeward side
of the trunk; the beautiful sandy beach at Westpunt. And I'd miss Henrik van Boven.

I also knew that Henrik and his mother would
think us cowardly if we left just because a few
German submarines were off Curaçao. I was awake
most of the night.

The next morning my father said that the Chinese
crews on the lake tankers that shuttled crude oil
across the sand bars at Maracaibo had refused to
sail without naval escorts. He said the refinery
would have to close down within a day, and that
meant precious gas and oil could not go to England,
or to General Montgomery in the African desert.

For seven days, not a ship moved by the Queen
Emma bridge, and there was gloom over Willemstad. The people had been very proud that the
little islands of Aruba and Curaçao were now among
the most important islands in the world; that vic-
tory or defeat depended on them. They were angry
with the Chinese crews, and on the third day, my

father said that mutiny charges had been placed against them.

"But," he said, "you must understand they are very frightened, and some of the people who are angry with them would not sail the little ships either."

He explained to me what it must feel like to ride the cargoes of crude oil, knowing that a torpedo or shell could turn the whole ship into flames any moment. Even though he wasn't a sailor, he volunteered to help man the lake tankers.

Soon, of course, we might also run out of fresh water. It rains very little in the Dutch West Indies unless there is a hurricane, and water from the few wells has a heavy salt content. The big tankers from the United States or England always carried fresh water to us in ballast, and then it was distilled again so that we could drink it. But now, all the big tankers were being held up in their ports until the submarines could be chased away.

Toward the end of the week, we began to run out of fresh vegetables because the schooner-men were also afraid. Now, my mother talked constantly about the submarines, the lack of water, and the shortage of food. It almost seemed that she was using the war as an excuse to leave Curaçao.

"The ships will be moving again soon," my father said confidently, and he was right.

I think it was February 21 that some of the Chinese sailors agreed to sail to Lake Maracaibo. But on that same day a Norwegian tanker, headed for Willemstad, was torpedoed off Curaçao, and fear again swept over the old city. Without our ships, we were helpless.

Then a day or two later, my father took me into the Schottegat where they were completing the loading of the S.S. *Empire Tern*, a big British tanker. She had machine guns fore and aft, one of the few armed ships in the harbor.

Although the trade wind was blowing, the smell of gas and oil lay heavy over the Schottegat. Other empty tankers were there, high out of the water, awaiting orders to sail once they had cargoes. The men on them were leaning over the rail watching all the activity on the *Empire Tern.*

I looked on as the thick hoses that were attached to her quivered when the gasoline was pumped into her tanks. The fumes shimmered in the air, and one by one, they "topped" her tanks, loading them right to the brim and securing them for sea. No one said very much. With all that aviation gasoline around, it was dangerous.

Then in the afternoon, we went to Punda and stood near the pontoon bridge as she steamed slowly down St. Anna Bay. Many others had come to watch, too, even the governor, and we all cheered as she passed, setting out on her lonely voyage to England. There, she would help refuel the Royal Air Force.

The sailors on the *Empire Tern*, which was painted

a dull white but had rust streaks all over her, waved back at us and held up their fingers in a V-for-victory sign.

We watched until the pilot boat, having picked up the harbor pilot from the *Empire Tern*, began to race back to Willemstad. Just as we were ready to go, there was an explosion and we looked toward the sea. The *Empire Tern* had vanished in a wall of red flames, and black smoke was beginning to boil into the sky.

Someone screamed, "There it is." We looked off to one side of the flames, about a mile away, and saw a black shape in the water, very low. It was a German submarine, surfaced now to watch the ship die.

A tug and several small motorboats headed out toward the *Tern*, but it was useless. Some of the women cried at the sight of her, and I saw men, my father included, with tears in their eyes. It didn't seem possible that only a few hours before I had been standing on her deck. I was no longer excited about the war; I had begun to understand that it meant death and destruction.

That same night, my mother told my father, "I'm taking Phillip back to Norfolk." I knew she'd made up her mind.

He was tired and disheartened over what had happened to the *Empire Tern*. He did not say much. But I do remember him saying, "Grace, I think you are making a mistake. You are both quite safe here in Scharloo." I wondered why he didn't simply order her to stay. But he wasn't that kind of a man.

The sunny days and dark, still nights passed slowly during March. The ships had begun to sail again, defying the submarines. Some were lost. Henrik and I often went down to Punda to watch them go out, hoping that they would be safe.

Neither my father nor my mother talked very much about us leaving. I thought that when two American destroyers arrived, along with the Dutch cruiser *Van Kingsbergen*, to protect the lake tankers, Mother would change her mind. But it only made her more nervous.

Then one day in early April, she said, "Your father has finally secured passage for us, so today will be your last day in school here, Phillip. We'll start packing tomorrow, and on Friday, we leave aboard a ship for Miami. Then we'll take the train to Norfolk."

Suddenly, I felt hollow inside. Then I became angry and accused her of being a coward. She told me to go off to school. I said I hated her.

All that day in school, I tried to think of what I could do. I thought about going somewhere and hiding until the ship had sailed, but on an island the size of Curaçao, there is no place to hide. Also, I knew it would cause my father trouble.

That night when he got home, I told him I wanted to stay with him. He smiled and put his long, thin arm around my shoulder. He said, "No, Phillip, I think it is best that you go with your mother. At a time like this, I can't be at home very much."

His voice seemed sad, although he was trying to be cheerful. He told me how wonderful it would be to return to the United States; how many things I had missed while we were on the island. I couldn't think of one.

Then I talked to my mother about staying on in Willemstad, and she became very upset with both of us. She said that we didn't love her and began to cry.

My father finally ended it by saying, "Phillip, the decision is made. You'll leave Friday with your mother."

So I packed, with her help, and said good-by to Henrik van Boven and the other boys. I told them we'd be gone just a short time; that we were going to visit my grandparents, my mother's parents, in Norfolk. But I had the feeling that it might be a very long time before I saw Curaçao and my father again.

Early Friday morning, we boarded the S.S. *Hato* in St. Anna Channel. She was a small Dutch freighter with a high bow and stern, and a bridge house in the middle between two well decks. I had seen her often in St. Anna Bay. Usually, she ran between Willemstad, Aruba, and Panama. She had a long stack and always puffed thick, black smoke.

In our cabin, which was on the starboard side and opened out to the boat deck, my father said, "Well, you can rest easy, Phillip. The Germans would never waste a torpedo on this old tub." Yet I saw him looking over the lifeboats. Then he inspected the fire hoses on the boat deck. I knew he was worried.

There were eight other passengers aboard, and they were all saying good-by to their relatives just as we were saying good-by to my father. In the tradition, people brought flowers and wine. It was almost like sailing in the days before the war, they told me.

Father was smiling and very gay but when the *Hato*'s whistle blasted out three times, meaning it was time to go, he said good-by to us between clenched teeth. I clung to him for a long time. Finally, he said, "Take good care of your mother."

I said I would.

We sailed down St. Anna Bay, and the Queen Emma bridge parted for us. Through watery eyes, I saw the fort and the old buildings of Punda and Otrabanda. Native schooners were beating in from the sea.

Then my mother pointed. I saw a tall man standing on the wall of Fort Amsterdam, waving at us. I knew it was my father. I'll never forget that tall, lonely figure standing on the sea wall.

The S.S. *Hato* took her first bite of open sea and began to pitch gently. We turned toward Panama, as we had to make a call there before proceeding to Miami. Down on the well decks, fore and aft, were four massive pumps that had to be delivered to Colón, the port at the Atlantic entrance to the Panama Canal.

I stayed out on deck for a long time, sitting by the lifeboat, looking back at Curaçao, feeling lonely and sad.

Finally my mother said, "Come inside now."

CHAPTER

Three

WE WERE TORPEDOED at about three o'clock in the morning on April 6, 1942, two days after leaving Panama.

I was thrown from the top bunk and suddenly found myself on my hands and knees on the deck. We could hear the ship's whistle blowing constantly, and there were sounds of metal wrenching and much shouting. The whole ship was shuddering. It felt as though we'd stopped and were dead in the water.

My mother was very calm, not at all like she was

at home. She talked quietly while she got dressed, telling me to tie my shoes, and be certain to carry my wool sweater, and to put on my leather jacket. Her hands were not shaking.

She helped me put on my life jacket, then put hers on, saying, "Now, remember everything that we were told about abandoning ship." The officers had held drills every day.

As she was speaking, there was another violent explosion. We were thrown against the cabin door, which the steward had warned us not to lock because it might become jammed. We pushed it open and went out to the boat deck, which was already beginning to tilt.

Everything was bright red, and there were great crackling noises. The entire afterpart of the ship was on fire, and sailors were launching the lifeboat that was on our deck. Steam lines had broken, and the steam was hissing out. Heat from the fire washed over us.

When the lifeboat had been swung out, the captain came down from the bridge. He was a small, wiry white-haired man and was acting the way I'd been told captains should act. He stood by the lifeboat in the fire's glow, very alert, giving orders to the crew. He was carrying a brief case and a navigation instrument I knew to be a sextant. On the other side of the ship, another lifeboat was being launched.

Near us, two sailors with axes chopped at lines, and two big life rafts plunged toward the water, which looked black except for pools of fire from burning fuel oil.

The captain shouted, "Get a move on! Passengers into the boats!" Tins of lubricating oil in the after-holds had ignited and were exploding, but the ones forward had not been exposed to the fire.

A sailor grabbed my mother's hand and helped her in, and then I felt myself being passed into the hands of a sailor on the boat. The other passengers were helped in, and someone yelled, "Lower away." At that moment, the *Hato* lurched heavily and something happened to the boat falls.

The bow tilted downward, and the next thing I knew we were all in the water. I saw my mother near me and yelled to her. Then something hit me from above.

A long time later (four hours I was told), I opened my eyes to see blue sky above. It moved back and forth, and I could hear the slap of water. I had a terrible pain in my head. I closed my eyes again, thinking maybe I was dreaming. Then a voice said, "Young bahss, how are you feelin'?"

I turned my head.

I saw a huge, very old Negro sitting on the raft near me. He was ugly. His nose was flat and his face was broad; his head was a mass of wiry gray hair. For a moment, I could not figure out where I was or who he was. Then I remembered seeing him working with the deck gang of the *Hato*.

I looked around for my mother, but there was no

one else on the raft. Just this huge Negro, myself, and a big black and gray cat that was licking his haunches.

The Negro said, "You 'ad a mos' terrible crack on d'ead, bahss. A strong-back glanc' offen your 'ead, an' I harl you board dis raff."

He crawled over toward me. His face couldn't have been blacker, or his teeth whiter. They made an alabaster trench in his mouth, and his pink-purple lips peeled back over them like the meat of a conch shell. He had a big welt, like a scar, on his left cheek. I knew he was West Indian. I had seen many of them in Willemstad, but he was the biggest one I'd ever seen.

I sat up, asking, "Where are we? Where is my mother?"

The Negro shook his head with a frown. "I true believe your mut-thur is safe an' soun' on a raff like dis. Or mebbe dey harl 'er into d'boat. I true believe dat."

Then he smiled at me, his face becoming less terrifying. "As to our veree location, I mus' guess we are somewhar roun' d'cays, somewhar mebbe fifteen latitude an' eighty long. We should 'ave pass dem til' dat mos' treacherous torpedo split d'veree hull. Two minute downg, at d'mos'."

I looked all around us. There was nothing but blue sea with occasional patches of orange-brown seaweed. No sight of the *Hato*, or other rafts, or boats. Just the sea and a few birds that wheeled over it. That lonely sea, and the sharp pains in my head, and the knowledge that I was here alone with a black man instead of my mother made me break into tears.

Finally the black man said, looking at me from bloodshot eyes, "Now, young bahss, I mos' feel like dat my own self, Timothy, but 'twould be of no particular use to do dat, eh?" His voice was rich calypso, soft and musical, the words rubbing off like velvet.

I felt a little better, but my head ached fiercely.

He nodded toward the cat. "Dis is Stew, d'cook's cat. He climb on d'raff, an' I 'ad no heart to trow 'im off." Stew was still busy licking. "'E got oi-ll all ovah hisself from d'wattah."

I looked closer at the black man. He was extremely old yet he seemed powerful. Muscles rippled over the ebony of his arms and around his shoulders. His chest was thick and his neck was the size of a small tree trunk. I looked at his hands and feet. The skin was alligatored and cracked, tough from age and walking barefoot on the hot decks of schooners and freighters.

He saw me examining him and said gently, "Put your 'ead back downg, young bahss, an' rest awhile longer. Do not look direct at d'sun. 'Tis too powerful."

I felt seasick and crawled to the side to vomit. He came up beside me, holding my head in his great clamshell hands. It didn't matter, at that moment, that he was black and ugly. He murmured, "Dis be good, dis be good."

When it was over, he helped me back to the center of the raft, saying, "'Tis mos' natural for you to do dis. 'Tis d'shock o' havin' all dis mos' terrible ting 'appen."

I then watched as he used his powerful arms and hands to rip up boards from the outside edges of the raft. He pounded them back together on cleats, forming two triangles; then he jammed the bases into slots between the raft boards. He stripped off his shirt and his pants, then demanded mine. I don't know what happened to my leather jacket or my sweater. But soon, we had a flimsy shelter from the burning sun.

Crawling under it to sprawl beside me, he said, "We 'ave rare good luck, young bahss. D'wattah kag did not bus' when d'raff was launch, an' we 'ave a few biscuit, some choclade, an' d'matches in d'tin is dry. So we 'ave rare good luck." He grinned at me then.

I was thinking that our luck wasn't so good. I was thinking about my mother on another boat or raft, not knowing I was all right. I was thinking about my father back in Willemstad. It was terrible not to be able to tell him where I was. He'd have boats and planes out within hours.

I guess the big Negro saw the look on my face. He said, "Do not be despair, young bahss. Someone will fin' us. Many schooner go by dis way, an' dis also be d'ship track to Jamaica, an' on."

After a bit, lulled by the bobbing of the raft and by the soft, pleasant sounds of the sea against the oil barrel floats, I went to sleep again. I was very tired and my head still ached. The piece of timber must have struck a glancing blow on the left side.

When I next awakened, it was late afternoon. The sun had edged down and the breeze across us was cool. But I felt very hot and the pain had not gone away. The Negro was sitting with his back toward me, humming something in calypso. His back was a great wall of black flesh, and I saw a cruel scar on one shoulder.

I asked, "What is your name?"

Hearing my voice, he turned with a wide grin. "Ah, you are back wit' me. It 'as been lonesome dese veree hours."

I repeated, "What is your name?"

"My own self? Timothy!"

"Your last name?"

He laughed, "I 'ave but one name. 'Tis Timothy."

"Mine is Phillip Enright, Timothy." My father had always taught me to address anyone I took to be an adult as "mister," but Timothy didn't seem to be a mister. Besides, he was black.

He said, "I knew a Phillip who feesh out of St. Jawn, but an outrageous mahn he was." He laughed deep inside himself.

I asked him for a drink of water.

He nodded agreeably, saying, "D'sun do parch."
He lifted a hinged section of the raft flooring and
drew out the keg, which was about two feet long.
There was a tin cup lashed to it. Careful not to
spill a drop, he said, "'Tis best to 'ave only an
outrageous smahl amount. Jus' enough to wet
d'tongue."

"Why?" I asked. "That is a large keg."

He scanned the barren sea and then looked back
at me, his old eyes growing remote. "D'large kag
'ave a way o' losin' its veree size."

"You said we would be picked up soon," I re-
minded him.

"Ah, yes," he said instantly, "but we mus' be wise
'bout what we 'ave."

I drank the tiny amount of water he'd poured
out and asked for more. He regarded me silently
a moment, then said, his eyes squinting, "A veree
lil' more, young bahss."

My lips were parched and my throat was dry. I
wanted a whole cup. "Please fill it up," I said.

Timothy poured only a few drops into the bottom.

"That isn't enough," I complained. I felt I could
drink three cups of it. But he pressed the wooden
stopper firmly back into the keg, ignoring me.

I said, "I must have water, Timothy. I'm very
hot."

Without answering, he opened the trap in the

raft and secured the keg again. It was then that I began to learn what a stubborn old man he could be. I began to dislike Timothy.

"Young bahss," he said, coming back under the shelter, "mebbe before d'night, a schooner will pass dis way, an' if dat 'appens, you may drink d'whole kag. Mebbe d'schooner will not pass dis way, so we mus' make our wattah last."

I said defiantly, "A schooner will find us. And my father has ships out looking for us."

Without even glancing at me, he answered, "True, young bahss." Then he closed his eyes and would not speak to me any more. He just sprawled out, a mound of silent black flesh.

I couldn't hold the tears back. I'm sure he heard me, but he didn't move a muscle of his face. Neither did he look up when I crawled out from under the shelter to get as far away from him as I could. I stayed on the edge of the raft for a long time, thinking about home and rubbing Stew Cat's back.

Although I hadn't thought so before, I was now beginning to believe that my mother was right. She didn't like them. She didn't like it when Henrik and I would go down to St. Anna Bay and play near the schooners. But it was always fun. The black people would laugh at us and toss us bananas or papayas.

She'd say, when she knew where we'd been, "They are not the same as you, Phillip. They are different and they live differently. That's the way it must be." Henrik, who'd grown up in Curaçao with them, couldn't understand why my mother felt this way.

I yelled over at him, "You're saving all the water for yourself."

I don't think he was asleep, but he didn't answer.

When the sky began to turn a deep blue, Timothy roused himself and looked around. He said, with just an unfriendly glance at me, "If luck be, d'flyin' feesh will flop on d'raff. We can save a few biscuit by eatin' d'feesh. Too, wattah is in d'feesh."

I was hungry but the thought of eating raw fish didn't appeal to me. I said nothing.

Just before dark, they began skimming across the water, their short, winglike fins taking them on flights of twenty or thirty feet, sometimes more.

A large one shot out of the water, skimmed toward us, and then slammed into the raft flooring. Timothy grabbed it, shouting happily. He rapped its head with his knife handle and tossed it beneath the shelter. Soon another came aboard, not so large. Timothy grabbed it, too.

Before total darkness, he had skinned them, deftly cutting meat from their sides. He handed me the two largest pieces. "Eat dem," he ordered.

I shook my head.

He looked at me in the fading light and said softly, "We will 'ave no other food tonight. You bes' eat dem, young bahss." With that, he pressed a piece of the fish against his teeth, sucking at it noisily.

Yes, they were different. They ate raw fish.

I turned away from him, over on my stomach. I thought about Curaçao, warm and safe; about our gabled house in Scharloo, and about my father. Suddenly I blamed my mother because I was on the raft with this stubborn old black man. It was all her fault. She'd wanted to leave the island.

I blurted out, "I wouldn't even be here with you if it wasn't for my mother."

I knew Timothy was staring at me through the darkness when he said, "She started dis terrible wahr, eh, young bahss?" He was a shadowy shape across the raft.

CHAPTER

Four

TOTAL DARKNESS blotted out the sea, and it became cold and damp. Timothy took the shelter down, and we both pulled our shirts and pants back on. They were stiff from salt and felt clammy. The wind picked up, blowing fine chill spray across the raft. Then the stars came out.

We stayed in the middle of the raft, side by side, as it drifted aimlessly over the sea. Stew Cat rubbed his back against the bottoms of my feet and then curled up down there. I was glad because he was warm.

I was thinking that it was very strange for me, a boy from Virginia, to be lying beside this giant Negro out on the ocean. And I guess maybe Timothy was thinking the same thing.

Once, our bodies touched. We both drew back, but I drew back faster. In Virginia, I knew they'd always lived in their sections of town, and us in ours. A few times, I'd gone down through the shacks of colored town with my father. They sold spicy crabs in one shack, I remember.

I saw them mostly in the summer, down by the river, fishing or swimming naked, but I didn't really know any of them. And in Willemstad, I didn't know them very well either. Henrik van Boven did, though, and he was much easier with them.

I asked, "Timothy, where is your home?"

"St. Thomas," he said. "Charlotte Amalie, on St. Thomas." He added, "'Tis a Virgin Islan'."

"Then you are American," I said. I remembered from school that we had bought the Virgins from Denmark.

He laughed. "I suppose, young bahss. I nevar gave it much thought. I sail all d'islan's, as well as Venezuela, Colombo, Panama. . . . I jus' nevar gave it much thought I was American."

I said, "Your parents were African, Timothy?"

He laughed, low and soft. "Young bahss, you want me to say I true come from Afre-ca?"

"You say what you want." It was just that Timothy looked very much like the men I'd seen in jungle pictures. Flat nose and heavy lips.

He shook his head. "I 'ave no recollection o' anythin' 'cept dese islan's. 'Tis pure outrageous, but I do not remember anythin' 'bout a place called Afre-ca."

I didn't know if he was telling the truth or not. He looked pure African. I said, "What about your mother?"

Now, there was deep laughter in his voice. "'Tis even more outrageous I do not remember a fatha or my mut-thur. I was raise by a woman call Hannah Gumbs. . . ."

"Then you are an orphan," I said.

"I guess, young bahss, I guess." He was chuckling to himself, rich and deep.

I looked over toward him, but again, he was just a shadowy shape, a large mound. "How old are you, Timothy?" I asked.

"Dat fact is also veree mysterious. Lil' more dan sixty, 'cause d'muscle in my legs b'speakin' to me, complain all d'time. But to be true, I do not know exact."

I was amazed that any man shouldn't know his own age. I was almost certain now that Timothy had indeed come from Africa, but I didn't tell him that. I said, "I'm almost twelve." I wanted him to know I was almost twelve so that he would stop treating me as though I were half that age.

"Dat is a veree important age," Timothy agreed. "Now, you mus' get some natural sleep. Tomorrow might be a veree long day, an' we 'ave much to do."

I laughed. There we were on that bucking raft with nothing to do except watch for schooners or aircraft. "What do we have to do?" I asked.

His eyes groped through the darkness for mine. He came up on his elbows. "Stay alive, young bahss, dat's what we 'ave to do."

Soon, it became very cold and I began shivering. Part of it was coldness, but there was also fear. If the raft tipped over, sharks would slash at us, I knew.

My head was aching violently again. During the day, the pain had been dull, but now it was shooting along both sides of my head. Once, sometime during the early night I felt his horny hand on my forehead. Then he shifted my body, placing it on the other side of him.

He murmured, "Young bahss, d'wind 'as shift. You'll be warmer on dis side."

I was still shivering, and soon he gathered me against him, and Stew Cat came back to be a warm ball against my feet. I could now smell Timothy, tucked up against him. He didn't smell like my father or my mother. Father always smelled of bay rum, the shaving lotion he used, and Mother smelled of some kind of perfume or cologne. Timothy smelled different and strong, like the black men who worked on the decks of the tankers when they were loading. After a while, I didn't mind the smell because Timothy's back was very warm.

The raft plunged on across the light swells throughout the long night.

I do not think he slept much during the night, but I'd been told that old people didn't sleep much anyway. I woke up when there was a pale band of light to the east, and Timothy said, "You fare well, young bahss? How is d'ead?"

"It still hurts," I admitted.

Timothy said, "A crack on d'ead takes a few days to go 'way." He opened the trap on the raft to pull out the water keg and the tin containing the biscuits, the chocolate squares, and dry matches.

I sat up, feeling dizzy. He allowed me half a cup of water and two hard biscuits, then fed Stew Cat with a wedge of leftover flying fish. We ate in silence as the light crept steadily over the smooth, oily sea. The wind had died and already the sun was beginning to scorch.

Timothy chewed slowly on half a biscuit. "Today, young bahss, a schooner will pass. I'd bet a jum on dat."

"I hope so," I said.

"I do tink we are not too far from Providencia an' San Andrés."

I looked hard at Timothy. "Are they islands?" He nodded.

I kept looking at him. It seemed there was a film,

a haze, separating us. I rubbed my eyes and opened them again. But the haze was still there. I glanced over at the red ball of sun, now clear of the horizon. It seemed dim. I said, "I think there is something wrong with my eyes."

Timothy said, "I warn you! You look direct at d'sun yestiddy."

Yes, that was it! I'd looked at the sun too much.

"Today," Timothy said, "do not eben look at d'wattah. D'glare is bad too."

He went about setting up the triangles for our shelter, and I took off my clothes. After he had draped my pants and shirt, I got under the shelter. The pain in my head was almost unbearable now, and I remember moaning. Timothy tore off a piece of his shirt from the shelter roof, soaked it in fresh water and placed it over my eyes. There was worry in his voice as he talked.

Awhile later, I took the cloth off my eyes and looked up. The inside of our shelter was shadowy and dark, but the pain had begun to go away. "It doesn't hurt as much any more," I said.

"Ah, see, it jus' takes time, young bahss."

I put the cool cloth back over my eyes and went to sleep again. When I woke up, it was night. Yet the air felt hot, and the breeze that came across the raft was warm. I lay there thinking.

"What time is it?" I asked.

"'Bout ten."

"At night?"

There was puzzlement in his voice. "'Tis day."

I put my hand in front of my face. Even in the very blackest night, you can see your own hand. But I could not see mine.

I screamed to Timothy, "I'm blind, I'm blind."

"What?" His voice was a frightened roar.

Then I knew he was bending over me. I felt his breath in my face. He said, "Young bahss, you cannot be blin'." He pulled me roughly from the shelter.

"Look at d'sun," he ordered. His hands pointed my face. I felt the strong warmth against it, but everything was black.

The silence seemed to last forever as he held my face toward the sun. Then a long, shuddering sigh came from his great body. He said, very gently, "Now, young bahss, you mus' lie downg an' rest. What 'as happen will go 'way. 'Tis all natural temporary." But his voice was hollow.

I got down on the hot boards, blinking my eyes again and again, trying to lift the curtain of blackness. I touched them. They did not feel any different. Then I realized that the pain had gone away. It had gone away but left me blind.

I could hear my voice saying, far off, "I don't feel any pain, Timothy. The pain has gone away."

I guess he was trying to think it all out. In a few minutes, he answered, "Once, ovah 'round Barbados, a mahn 'ad an outrageous crack on d'ead when a sailin' boom shift. Dis mahn was blin' too. Tree whole day 'e saw d'night. Den it true went away."

"Do you think that is what will happen to me?"

"I tink dat be true, young bahss," he said.

Then he became very quiet.

After a moment, lying there in darkness, hearing the creak of the raft and feeling its motion, it all hit me. I was blind and we were lost at sea.

I began to crawl, screaming for my mother and my father, but felt his hard hands on my arms. He held me tight and said, low and soft, "Young bahss, young bahss." He kept repeating it.

I'll never forget that first hour of knowing I was blind. I was so frightened that it was hard for me to breathe. It was as if I'd been put inside something that was all dark and I couldn't get out.

I remember that at one point my fear turned to anger. Anger at Timothy for not letting me stay in the water with my mother, and anger at her because I was on the raft. I began hitting him and I remember him saying, "If dat will make you bettah, go 'ead."

After a while, I felt very tired and fell back on the hot boards.

CHAPTER

Five

I GUESS IT WAS TOWARD NOON on the third day aboard the raft that Timothy said tensely, "I 'ear a motah."

"A motah?"

"Sssssh."

I listened. Yes, there was a far-off engine sound coming in faintly above the slap of the sea. Then I could hear Timothy moving around. "'Tis an aircraft," he said.

My heart began to pound. *They were looking for*

us. I felt around, then crawled from beneath the shelter to look toward the sound. But I could see nothing.

I heard the hinges on the trap door creak. Timothy said quietly, as though afraid to chase the sound away, "It knowin' what we doin' 'ere by seein' smoke, I do believe."

He ripped down one of the triangle legs, and I heard cloth tearing. Soon he said, "We made d'torch, young bahss. D'mahn up dere be seein' d'smoke all right, all right."

The faint drone of the aircraft seemed closer now. In a moment, I smelled cloth burning and knew he was holding the wrapped piece of wood toward the sky.

He shouted, "Look downg 'ere."

But already the drone seemed to be fading.

Timothy yelled, "I see it, I see it! Way to port!"

I tried to make my eyes cut through the darkness. "Is he coming our way?"

"Don' know, don' know, young bahss," Timothy replied anxiously.

I said, "I can't hear it now." There was nothing in the air but the sea sounds.

Timothy shouted, "Look downg 'ere! Dere is a raff wit a lil' blin' boy, an' old mahn, an' Stew Cat. Look downg 'ere, I tell you."

The drone could not be heard. Just the slap of the water and the sound of the light wind making our shelter flap.

We were alone again on the ocean.

After a moment of silence, I heard the sizzle of the water as Timothy doused the torch. He sighed deeply, "I be ready next time for true. Let d'torch dry, den I be ready."

Soon he sat down beside me. "'Tis a good ting not to harass d'soul ovah dis. We are edgin' into d'aircraft track, same as d'ship dey run."

I said nothing but put my head down on my knees.

"Do not be dishearten, young bahss. Today, we will be foun', to be true."

But the long, hot day was passing without sight of anything. I knew Timothy was constantly scanning the sea. It was all so calm now that the raft didn't even seem to be drifting. Once, I crawled over to the edge to touch the warm water and felt Timothy right behind me.

He said, "Careful, young bahss. D'sharks always hungry, always waitin' for d'mahn to fall ovah-board."

Drawing back from the edge, I asked, "Are there many here?"

"Yes, many 'ere. But long as we 'ave our raff, they do not meliss us."

Standing on the sea wall at Willemstad, some-times I'd seen their fins in the water. I'd also seen them on the dock at the Ruyterkade market, their mouths open and those sharp teeth grinning.

I went back under the shelter, spending a long

time rubbing Stew Cat. He purred and pushed himself along my body. I was glad that I had seen him and had seen Timothy before going blind. I thought how awful it would have been to awaken on the raft and not know what they looked like.

Timothy must have been standing over us, for he said, "D'cot not good luck." After a moment he added, "But to cause d'death of a cot is veree bad luck."

"I don't think Stew Cat is bad luck," I said. "I'm glad he is here with us."

Timothy did not answer, but turned back, I guess, to watch the sea again. I could imagine those bloodshot eyes, set in that massive, scarred black face, sweeping over the sea.

"Tell me what's out there, Timothy," I said. It was very important to know that now. I wanted to know everything that was out there.

He laughed. "Jus' miles o' blue wattah, miles o' blue wattah."

"Nothing else?"

He realized what I meant. "Oh, to be sure, young bahss, I see a feesh jump way fo'ward. Dat mean large feesh chase 'im. Den awhile back, a turtle pass us port side, but too far out to reach 'im back. . . ."

His eyes were becoming mine. "What's in the sky, Timothy?"

"In d'sky?" He searched it. "No clouds, young

bahss, jus' blue like 'twas yestiddy. But now an' den, I see a petrel. While ago, a booby . . ."

I laughed for the first time all day. It was a funny name for a bird. "A booby?"

Timothy was quite serious. "Dis booby I saw was a blue face, mebbe nestin' out o' Serranilla Bank, mebbe not. Dey be feedin' on d'flyin' feesh. I true watchin' d'birds 'cause dey tell us we veree close to d'shore."

"How does a booby look, Timothy?"

"Nothin' much," he replied. "Tail like our choclade, sharp beak, mos' white on 'is body."

I tried to picture it, wondering if I'd ever see a bird again.

CHAPTER

Six

IN THE EARLY MORNING (I knew it was early because the air was still cool and there was dampness on the boards of the raft), I heard Timothy shout, "I see an islan', true."

In wild excitement, I stumbled up and fell overboard.

I went under the water, yelling for him, then came up, gasping. I heard a splash and knew he was in the water too.

Something slapped up against my leg, and I

thought it was Timothy. I knew how to swim, but didn't know which way to go. So I was treading water. Then I heard Timothy's frightened roar, "Sharks," and he was thrashing about near me.

He grabbed my hair with one hand and used his other arm to drag me back toward the raft. I had turned on my face and was trying to hold my breath. Then I felt my body being thrown, and I was back on the boards of the raft, gasping for air. I knew that Timothy was still in the water because I could hear splashing and cursing.

The raft tilted down suddenly on one side. Timothy was back aboard. Panting, he bent over me. He yelled, "Damn fool mahn! I tol' you 'bout d'shark!"

I knew Timothy was in a rage. I could hear his heavy breathing and knew he was staring at me. "Shark all 'round us, all d'time," he roared.

I said, "I'm sorry."

Timothy said, "On dis raff, you crawl, young bahss. You 'ear me?"

I nodded. His voice was thick with anger, but in a moment, after he took several deep breaths, he asked, "You all right, young bahss?"

I guess he sat down beside me to rest. His breathing was still heavy. Finally, he said, "Mahn die quick out dere."

We'd both forgotten about the island. I said, "Timothy, you saw an island!"

He laughed. "Yes, d'islan'! Dere 'tis. . . ."

I said, "Where?"

Timothy answered scornfully, "Dere, look, mahn, look . . ."

Angrily, I said to him, "I can't see." He kept forgetting that.

His voice was low when he said, "Yes, young bahss. Dat be true! In all dis harassment wid d'shark, I did forget."

Then I felt his hands on my shoulders. He twisted them. "Dat direction, young bahss."

Straining to look where he had me pointed, I asked, "Are there any people on it?"

"'Tis a veree smahl islan', outrageous low."

I repeated, "Are there any people on it?" I thought they could contact my father and then send for help.

Timothy answered honestly, "No, young bahss. No people. People not be libin' on d'islan' dat 'as no wattah."

No people. No water. No food. No phones. It was not any better than the raft. In fact, it might be worse. "How far away are we?"

"'Bout two mile," Timothy said.

"Maybe we should stay on the raft. A schooner will see us, or an airplane."

Timothy said positively, "No, we bettah off on lan'. An' we driftin' dat way. D'tide be runnin' wid us." His voice was happy. He wanted to be off the sea.

I was certain my father had planes and ships out

looking for us. I said, "Timothy, the Navy is searching for us. I know."

Timothy did not answer me. He just said, "'Tis a pretty ting, to be sure. I see a white beach, an' behin' dat, low sea-grape bushes; den on d'hill, some palm. Mebbe twenty, thirty palm."

I was sure he couldn't even see that far.

I said, "Timothy, wouldn't it be better if we stayed on the raft and found a big island with people on it?"

He ignored me. He said, "Bidin' d'night, I saw surf washin' white ovah banks off to port, but did not awaken you, young bahss. But knew we be gettin' near d'cays. . . ."

I said, "I don't want to go on that island."

I don't think there was anyone on earth as stubborn as old Timothy. There was steel in his voice when he answered, "We be goin' on dat islan', young bahss. Dat be true."

But he knew how I felt now, because he added, "From dis islan', we will get help. Be true, I swear. . . ."

CHAPTER

Seven

IT SEEMED HOURS but it was probably only one until Timothy said, "Do not be alarm now, young bahss. I am goin' to jump into d'wattah an' kick dis raff to d'shore. Widout dat, we'll pass d'islan', by-'n'-by."

In a moment, I heard a splash on one side of the raft and then Timothy's feet began drumming the water. I guess he was not afraid of sharks this close in. Soon, he yelled, "Boddam, young bahss, boddam." His feet had touched sand. In another few minutes, the raft lurched and I knew it had grounded.

I listened for sounds from shore, hoping there would be a cheerful "hello," but there were none. Just the wash of the low surf around the raft.

Timothy said, "'Ere, young bahss, on my shoulders an' I'll fetch you to d'lan'." He helped me to his back.

I said, "Don't forget Stew Cat."

He laughed back heartily. "One at a time, young bahss."

With me on his back, he splashed ashore, and judging from the time it took, the raft wasn't very far out. Then he lifted me down again.

"Lan'," he shouted.

The warm sand did feel good on my feet, and now I was almost glad that we wouldn't have to spend another night on the hard, wet boards of the raft.

He said, "Touch it, young bahss. Feel d'lan', 'tis outrageous good."

I reached down. The grains of sand felt very fine, almost like powder.

Timothy said, "'Tis a beautiful cay, dis cay. Nevah hab I seen dis cay." Then he led me to sit under a clump of bushes. He said, "You res' easy while I pull d'raff more out of d'wattah. We mus' not lose it."

I sat there in the shade, running sand through

my fingers, wondering where, among all those many islands in the Caribbean, we were.

Timothy shouted up from the water, "Many feesh 'ere. *Langosta,* too, I b'knowin'. We ros' dem."

Langosta, I knew, was the native lobster, the one without claws. I heard Timothy splashing around down by the surf and knew he was pulling the raft up as far as he could get it.

A moment later, puffing hard, he flopped down beside me. He said, "Cotch me breath, den I will tour d'islan', an' select a place for d'camp. . . ."

He put Stew Cat into my lap.

"Camp?" I asked, stroking big Stew.

Timothy replied, "We mebbe 'ere two, tree days. So we be libin' comfortable."

He could tell I was discouraged because we had come to the island and there were no people on it. He said confidently, "We be rescue, true. Before d'night, I build a great fire pile o' brush an' wood. So d'nex' aircraft dat fly ovah, we set it off."

"Where are we, Timothy? Near Panama?"

He answered slowly, "I cannot be sure, young bahss. Not veree sure."

"But you said you knew about the banks and the cays that are near the banks." I wondered if he knew anything, really, or if he was just a stupid old black man.

Timothy said, "Lissen, I know dat many banks an' cays are roun' fifteen north an' eighty long. Dere is Roncador an' Serranno; Quito Sueño an' Ser-

ranilla an' Rosalind; den dere is Beacon an' North
Cay. Off to d'wes', somewhere, is Providencia an'
San Andrés . . ." He paused a moment and then
said, "Far 'way, up dere, I tink, is d'Caymens, an'
den Jamaica."

"But you are not sure of this island?"

Timothy answered gravely, "True, I am not sure."

"Do the schooners usually come close by here?"
I asked.

Again very gravely, Timothy said, "D'mahn who
feeshes follows d'feesh. Sartainly, d'feesh be 'ere. I
be seein' wid my own self eyes."

I kept feeling that Timothy was holding something back from me. It was the tone of his voice.
I'd heard my father talk that way a few times. Once,
when he didn't want to tell me my grandfather was
about to die; another time was when a car ran over
my dog in Virginia.

Of course, both times happened when I was
younger. Now, my father was always honest with
me, I thought, because he said that in the end that
was better. I wished Timothy would be honest with
me.

Instead he got up to take a walk around the cay,
saying he'd be back in a few minutes. Then Stew
Cat wandered away. I called to him but he seemed
to be exploring too. Realizing that I was alone on
the beach I became frightened.

I knew how helpless I was without Timothy. First
I began calling for Stew Cat but when he didn't

return I began shouting for Timothy. There was no answer. I wondered if he'd fallen down and was hurt. I began to crawl along the beach and ran head on into a clump of low hanging brush.

I sat down again, batting at gnats that were buzzing around my face. Something brushed against my arm, and I yelled out in terror. But I heard a meow and knew it was only Stew Cat. I reached for him and held him tight until I heard brush crackling and sang out, "Timothy?"

"Yes, young bahss," he called back from quite a distance.

When he was closer, I said harshly, "Never leave me again. Don't you ever leave me again!"

He laughed. "Dere is nothin' to fear 'ere. I walked roun' d'whole islan', an' dere is nothin' but sea grape, sand, a few lil' lizzard, an' dose palm tree . . ."

I repeated, "Never leave me alone, Timothy."

"All right, young bahss, I promise," he said.

He must have been looking all around, for he said, "No wattah 'ere, but 'tis no problem. We still 'ave wattah in d'kag, an' we will trap more on d'firs' rain."

Still believing he wasn't telling me everything, I said, "You were gone a long time."

He answered uneasily, "Thirty minutes at mos'. D'islan' is 'bout one mile long, an' a half wide, shaped like d'melon. I foun' a place to make our camp, up near d'palm. 'Twill be a good place for a lookout. D'rise is 'bout forty feet from d'sea."

I nodded, then said, "I'm hungry, Timothy."

We were both hungry. He went back to the raft, took out the keg of water and the tin of biscuits and chocolate.

While we were eating, I said, "You are worried about something, Timothy. Please tell me the truth. I'm old enough to know."

Timothy waited a long time before answering, probably trying to choose the right words. Finally, he said, "Young bahss, dere is, in dis part of d'sea, a few lil' cays like dis one, surround on bot' sides by hombug banks. Dey are cut off from d'res' o' d'sea by dese banks. . . ."

I tried to make a mental picture of that. Several small islands tucked up inside great banks of coral that made navigation dangerous was what I finally decided on.

"You think we are on one of those cays?"

"Mebbe, young bahss, mebbe."

Fear coming back to me—I knew he'd made a mistake in bringing us ashore—I said, "Then no ships will pass even close to us. Not even schooners! We're trapped here!" We might live here forever, I thought.

Again he did not answer directly. I was beginning to learn that he had a way of being honest while still being dishonest. He said, "D'place I am tinking of is call Debil's Mout'. 'Tis a U-shaped ting, wit dese sharp coral banks on either side, runnin' maybe forty, fifty mile. . . ."

He let that sink in. It sounded bad. But then he said, "I do hope, young bahss, dat I am outrageous mistaken."

"If we are in the Devil's Mouth, how can we be rescued?" I asked angrily. It was his fault we were there.

"D'fire pile! When aircraft fly above, dey will see d'smoke an' fire!"

"But they might just think it is a native fisherman. No one else would come here!"

I could picture him nodding, thinking about that. Finally, he said, "True, but we cannot fret 'bout it, can we? We'll make camp, an' see what 'appens."

He poured me a half cup of water, saying happily, "Since we 'ave made lan', we can celebrate."

I drank it slowly and thoughtfully.

CHAPTER

Eight

DURING THE AFTERNOON, Timothy was busy and we did not talk much. He was making a hut of dried palm fronds. I sat near him under a palm. Now that we were on shore, I again began to think about what had happened to my mother. Somehow, I felt she was safe. I was also sure that a search had been started for us, not fully understanding that a war was on and that all the ships and aircraft were needed to fight the U-boats. I even thought about

Henrik van Boven and what a story I would have
to tell when I saw him again.

I tried not to think about my eyes, sitting there
under the palm, listening to Timothy hum as he
made the camp. I trusted him that my sight would
return within a few days. I also trusted him that an
aircraft would spot our fire pile.

In late afternoon, he said proudly, "Look, our
hut!"

I had to remind him again, stupid old man, that
I couldn't see, so he took my hands and ran them
over the fronds. It was a hut, he said, about eight
feet wide and six feet deep, with supports made of
wood he'd picked off the beach. The supports were
tied together with strong vines that covered the
north end of the island.

The roof, which sloped back, he said, was about
six feet off the ground. I could easily stand up in
it, but Timothy couldn't. Not quite.

Timothy said, "Tomorrow, we be gettin' mats to
sleep on, weave our own, but tonight we mus' sleep
on d'sand. 'Tis soft."

I knew he was very proud of the hut. It had
taken him only a few hours to build it.

"Now," he said, "I mus' go downg to d'reef an'
fetch langosta. We'll ros' it, to be true."

I became frightened again the minute he said
it. I didn't want to be left alone, and I was afraid
something might happen to him. "Take me with you,
Timothy," I pleaded.

"Not on d'reef," he answered firmly. "I 'ave not been dere before. If 'tis safe, tomorrow I will take you." With that, he went down the hill without saying another word.

My mother was right, I thought. They had their place and we had ours. He did not really like me, or he would have taken me along. He was different.

It seemed as though he were gone for a very long time. Once, I thought I heard an aircraft, but it was probably just my imagination. I began yelling for Timothy to come back, but I guess he couldn't hear because of water noise on the reef.

The palm fronds above me rattled in the breeze, and there were other noises from the underbrush. I knew Stew Cat was around somewhere, but it didn't sound like him.

I wondered if Timothy had checked for snakes. There were also scorpions on most Caribbean islands, and they were deadly. I wondered if there were any on our cay.

During those first few days on the island, the times I spent alone were terrible. It was, of course, being unable to see that made all the sounds so frightening. I guess if you are born blind, it is not so bad. You grow up knowing each sound and what it means.

Suddenly, the tears came out. I knew it was not a manly thing to do, something my father would have frowned on, but I couldn't stop. Then from nowhere came Stew Cat. He rubbed along my arms and up against my cheek, purring hard. I held him close.

Soon, Timothy came up the hill, shouting, "Young bahss, tree nice langosta."

I refused to speak to him because he had left me for such a long time.

He stood over me and said, "'Ere, touch dem, dey are still alive." He was almost crowing over his lobster.

I turned away. Sooner or later, Timothy would have to understand that he could not ignore me one minute and then treat me as a friend the next.

He said softly, "Young bahss, be an outrageous mahn if you like, but 'ere I'm all you got."

I didn't answer.

He roasted the langosta over the fire, and later we crawled into the hut to spend our first night on the silent island.

Timothy seemed very tired and groaned a lot. Before we went to sleep, I asked him, "Tell me the truth, Timothy, how old are you?"

He sighed deeply, "More dan seventy. Eben more dan seventy. . . ."

He was very old. Old enough to die there.

In the morning, Timothy began making the fire pile down on the beach. He had a plan. We'd always keep a small fire smoldering up by the hut, and if an airplane came near, he'd take a piece of burning wood from our small fire to ignite the big one. That

way, he said, we could save the few matches that
we had.

It didn't take him long to stack driftwood over
dried palm fronds. Then he said, "Now, young
bahss, we mus' say somethin' on d'san'."

Sometimes it was difficult to understand Timothy.
The soft and beautiful West Indian accent and
way of speaking weren't always clear.

"Say something on the sand?" I asked.

"So dey be knowin' we are downg 'ere," he explained patiently.

"Who?"

"D'mahn in d'sky, of course."

"Oh." Now I understood.

I guess Timothy was standing there looking at me,
waiting for me to say something or do something. I
heard him say, "Well, young bahss."

"What do we do now?" I asked.

His voice now impatient, he said, "Say somethin'
wid d'rock, wid many rock; eeevery rock be sayin'
somethin'. . . ."

I frowned at him. "I don't think I can help you,
Timothy. I can't see any rocks."

Timothy groaned. "I can see d'rock, young bahss.
But what do we say?"

I laughed at him, enjoying it now. "We say
'help.'"

He grunted satisfaction.

For the next twenty or thirty minutes, I could
hear Timothy dropping rocks against each other,

singing softly to himself in calypso. It was a song about "fungee an' feesh." I'd had "fungi" in Willemstad down in the blacks' market at Ruyterkade. It was just plain old corn meal. But most food has different names in the islands.

Soon, he came to stand over me. "Now, young bahss," he said. He seemed to be waiting.

"Yes?"

There was a silence until Timothy broke it with anguish. "Wid d'rock, say 'help.'"

I looked up in his direction and suddenly understood that Timothy could not spell. He was just too stubborn, or too proud, to admit it.

I nodded and began feeling around the sand for a stick.

He asked, "What you reachin' for?"

"A stick to make lines with."

He placed one in my hands, and I carefully lettered H-E-L-P on the sand while he stood above me, watching. He kept murmuring, "Ah-huh, ah-huh," as if making sure I was spelling it correctly.

When I had finished, Timothy said approvingly, "I tell you, young bahss, dat do say help." Then he happily arranged the rocks on the sand, following my lines.

I felt good. I knew how to do something that Timothy couldn't do. *He couldn't spell.* I felt superior to Timothy that day, but I let him play his little game, pretending not to know that he really couldn't spell.

CHAPTER
Nine

IN THE AFTERNOON, Timothy said we'd make a rope.

On the north end of the island, tough vines, almost as large as a pencil, were laced over the sand. It took us several hours to tear out a big pile of them. Then Timothy began weaving a rope that would stretch all the way down the hill to the beach and fire pile.

The rope was for me. If he happened to be out on the reef, and I heard a plane, I could take a light from our campfire, follow the rope down, and touch off the big fire. The vine rope would also serve to get me safely down to the beach.

After we'd torn the vines out, and he was weaving the rope, he said, "Young bahss, you mus' begin to help wid d'udder wark."

We were sitting up by the hut. I had my back to a palm and was thinking that back in Willemstad, at this moment, I'd probably be sitting in a classroom, three desks away from Henrik, listening to Herr Jonckheer talk about European history. I'd been tutored in Dutch the first year in Willemstad so I could attend the regular school. Now I could speak it and understand it.

My hands were tired from pulling the vines, and I just wanted to sit and think. I didn't want to work. I said, "Timothy, I'm blind. I can't see to work."

I heard him cutting something with his sharp knife. He replied softly, "D'han' is not blin'."

Didn't the old man understand? To work, aside from pulling up vines or drawing something in the sand, you must be able to see.

Stubbornly, he said, "Young bahss, we need sleepin' mats. You can make d'mats."

I looked over in his direction. "You do it," I said.

He sighed back, saying, "D'best matmaker in Charlotte Amalie, downg in Frenchtown, b'total blin'."

"But he's a man, and he has to do that to make a living."

"B'true," Timothy said quietly.

But in a few minutes, he placed several lengths of palm fiber across my lap. He really was a black mule. "D'palm mat is veree easy. Jus' ovah an' under . . ."

Becoming angry with him, I said, "I tell you, I can't see."

He paid no attention to me. "Take dis' han' hol' d'palm like dis; den ovah an' under, like d'mahn in Frenchtown; den more palm."

I could feel him standing there watching me as I tried to reeve the lengths, but I knew they weren't fitting together. He said, "Like dis, I tell you," and reached down to guide my hand. "Ovah an' under . . ."

I tried again, but it didn't work. I stood up, threw the palm fibers at him, and screamed, "You ugly black man! I won't do it! You're stupid, you can't even spell . . ."

Timothy's heavy hand struck my face sharply.

Stunned, I touched my face where he'd hit me. Then I turned away from where I thought he was. My cheek stung, but I wouldn't let him see me with tears in my eyes.

I heard him saying very gently, "B'gettin' back to wark, my own self."

I sat down again.

He began to sing that "fungee and feesh" song in a low voice, and I could picture him sitting on the sand in front of the hut; that tangled gray hair, the ugly black face with the thick lips, those great horny hands winding the strands of vine.

The rope, I thought. It wasn't for him. It was for me.

After a while, I said, "Timothy . . ."

He did not answer, but walked over to me, pressing more palm fronds into my hands. He murmured, "'Tis veree easy, ovah an' under . . ." Then he went back to singing about fungee and feesh.

Something happened to me that day on the cay. I'm not quite sure what it was even now, but I had begun to change.

I said to Timothy, "I want to be your friend."

He said softly, "Young bahss, you 'ave always been my friend."

I said, "Can you call me Phillip instead of young boss?"

"Phill-eep," he said warmly.

CHAPTER

Ten

URING OUR SEVENTH NIGHT on the island, it rained. It was one of those tropical storms that comes up swiftly without warning. We were asleep on the palm mats that I'd made, but it awakened us immediately. The rain sounded like bullets hitting on the dried palm frond roof. We ran out into it, shouting and letting the fresh water hit our bodies. It was cool and felt good.

Timothy yelled that his catchment was working. He had taken more boards from the top of the raft and had made a large trough that would catch the rain. He'd picked up bamboo lengths on the beach and had fitted them together into a short pipe to funnel the rain water into our ten-gallon keg.

It rained for almost two hours, and Timothy was quite angry with himself for not making a second catchment because the keg was soon filled and over-flowing.

We stayed out in the cool rain for twenty or thirty minutes and then went back inside. The roof leaked badly but we didn't mind. We got on our mats and opened our mouths to the sweet, fresh water. Stew Cat was huddled in a miserable ball over in a corner, Timothy said, not enjoying it at all.

I liked the rain because it was something I could hear and feel; not something I must see. It peppered in bursts against the frond roof, and I could hear the drips as it leaked through. The squall wind was in the tops of the palms and I could imagine how they looked in the night sky, thrashing against each other high over our little cay.

I wanted it to rain all night.

We talked for a long time when the rain began to slack off. Timothy asked me about my mother and father. I told him all about them and about how we lived in Scharloo, getting very lonesome and homesick while I was telling him. He kept saying, "Ah, dat be true?"

Then Timothy told me what he could remember from his own childhood. It wasn't at all like mine.

He'd never gone to school, and was working on a fishing boat by the time he was ten. It almost seemed the only fun he had was once a year at carnival when he'd put frangipani leaves around his ankles and dress up in a donkey hide to parade around with *mocki jumbis,* the spirit chasers, while the old ladies of Charlotte Amalie danced the *bambola* around them.

He chuckled. "I drink plenty rhum dose tree days of carnival."

I could picture him in his donkey skin, wheeling around to the music of the steel bands. They had them in Willemstad too.

Because it had been on my mind I told him that my mother didn't like black people and asked him why.

He answered slowly, "I don' like some white people my own self, but 'twould be outrageous if I didn' like any o' dem."

Wanting to hear it from Timothy, I asked him why there were different colors of skin, white and black, brown and red, and he laughed back, "Why b'feesh different color, or flower b'different color? I true don' know, Phill-eep, but I true tink beneath d'skin is all d'same."

Herr Jonckheer had said something like that in school but it did not mean quite as much as when Timothy said it.

Long after he'd begun to snore in the dripping hut, I thought about it. Suddenly, I wished my

father and mother could see us there together on
the little island.

I moved close to Timothy's big body before I
went to sleep. I remember smiling in the darkness.
He felt neither white nor black.

In the morning, the air was crisp and the cay
smelled fresh and clean. Timothy cooked a small
fish, a pompano, that he'd speared at dawn down
on the reef. Neither of us had felt so good or so
clean since we had been aboard the *Hato*. And
without discussing it, we both thought this might
be the day an aircraft would swing up into the
Devil's Mouth, if that's where we were.

The pompano, broiled over the low fire, tasted
good. Of course, we were eating little but what
came from the sea. Fish, langosta, mussels, or the
eggs from sea urchins, those small, black round sea
animals with sharp spines that attach themselves
to the reefs.

Timothy had tried to make a stew from seaweed
but it tasted bitter. Then he'd tried to boil some
new sea-grape roots but they made us ill. The only
thing that ever worked for him was sea-grape leaves,
boiled first in sea water and then cooked in fresh
water.

But above us, forty feet from the ground, Timothy
said, was a feast. Big, fat green coconuts. When
we'd landed, there were a few dried ones on the
ground, but the meat in them was not very tasty.

In a fresher one, there was still some milk, but it was rancid.

At least once a day, especially when we were around the hut, Timothy would say, "'Tis outrageous dem coconut hang up in d'sky when we could use d'milk an' meat." Or he'd say, "Timothy, my own self, long ago could climb d'palm veree easy." Or hinting, and I guess looking up at them, "Phill-eep, I do believe you b'gettin' outrageous strong 'ere on d'islan'."

He made a point of saying that if he were only fifty again, he could climb the tree and slice them off with his knife. But at seventy-odd, he did not think he could make it to the top.

That morning over breakfast, Timothy said, looking to the tops of the palms, I'm sure, "A lil' milk from d'coconut would b'good now, eh, Phill-eep?"

As yet, I didn't have the courage to climb the palms. "Yes, it would," I said.

Timothy cleared his throat, sighed deeply, and put the coconuts out of his mind. But I knew he'd try me again.

He said, "Dem devilin' coconuts aside, your mutthur would never be knowin' you now."

I asked why.

"You are veree brown an' veree lean," he said.

I tried to imagine how I looked. I knew my shirt and pants were in tatters. My hair felt ropy. There was no way to comb it. I wondered how my eyes looked and asked Timothy about that.

"Dey look widout cease," he said. "Dey stare, Phill-eep."

"Do they bother you?"

Timothy laughed. "Not me. Eeevery day I tink what rare good luck I 'ave dat you be 'ere wid my own self on dis outrageous, hombug islan'."

I thought awhile and then asked him, "How long was it before that friend of yours, that friend in the Barbados, could see again?"

Timothy replied vaguely, "Oh, many mont', I do recall."

"But you told me on the raft it was only three days."

"Did I say dat?"

"Yes!"

"Well," Timothy said, "'twas a long time ago. But 'e got 'is sight back, to be true." He paused a moment, then said, "Now, I tell you, we got much wark to do today."

I noticed more and more that Timothy always changed the subject when we began to talk about my eyes. He would make any kind of an excuse.

"What work?" I asked.

"Now, lemme see," he said. "For one ting, we mus' make another catchment . . . an' we mus' go to d'reef for food . . . an' . . ."

I waited.

Timothy finally exploded. "Now, dat is a lot o' wark, Phill-eep, to be true."

CHAPTER

Eleven

TIMOTHY HAD FASHIONED A CANE for me, and I was now using it to feel my way around the island. I fell down often, but unless I fell into sea grape, it did not hurt. Even then, I only got a few scratches.

Slowly, I was beginning to know the island. By myself, keeping my feet in the damp sand, which meant I was near the water, I walked the whole way around it. Timothy was very proud of me.

From walking over it, feeling it, and listening to it, I think I knew what our cay looked like. As

Timothy said, it was shaped like a melon, or a turtle, sloped up from the sea to our ridge where the palms flapped all day and night in the light trade wind.

The beach, I now believed, was about forty yards wide in most places, stretching all the way around the island. On one end, to the east, was a low coral reef that extended several hundred yards, awash in many places.

I know it was to the east because one morning I was down there with Timothy when the sun came up, and I could feel the warmth on my face from that direction.

The sea grape, a few feet tall at the edge of the beach, and higher farther back, grew along the slopes of the hill on all sides. There was also some other brush that did not feel like sea grape, but Timothy did not know the name of it.

To the south, the beach sloped gradually out into the water. On the north side, it was different. There were submerged coral reefs and great shelves. The water became deep very abruptly. Timothy warned against going into the water here because the sharks could swim close to shore.

Timothy said that the water all around the cay was clear and that he could see many beautiful fish. There was brain coral and organ-pipe coral that the parrot fish would nibble.

From what I could feel and hear, our cay seemed a lovely island and I wished that I could see it. I planned to walk around it at least once a day, following the vine rope from the ridge to the beach, then setting out along the sand.

I was starting to be less dependent on the vine rope, and sometimes it seemed to me that Timothy was trying hard to make me independent of him. I thought I knew why, but I did not talk to him about it. I did not want to think about the possibility of Timothy dying and leaving me alone on the cay.

Because the rain the night before had made us hopeful, I think both of us did our chores with one ear to the sky, listening for the sound of engines. But all day we heard nothing but familiar sounds, the surf, the wind, and the cries of sea birds.

That night after dinner, Timothy grumbled, "No aircraft! D'islan' mus' 'ave a jumbi."

"Don't talk nonsense, Timothy," I said.

"D'evil spirit harass an' meliss us," he said darkly. "An' we do not 'ave a chicken or grains o' corn to chase 'im."

I said, "Timothy, you can't really believe in that."

My father had told me about "obediah," or "voodoo," in the West Indies. It had come over from Africa, of course. Haiti was the worst of all for it, but there was some practice on all the islands. It was mixed up with religion and witch doctors.

I knew he was looking at Stew Cat when he said, "Mebbe dat outrageous cat is d'jumbi."

"He's just an old cat, Timothy," I protested.

Recalling everything that had happened, Timothy said, "He came board d'raff, an' we got separated from all else; den d'young bahss' eyes got dark, gibbin' us exceedin' trouble; den we float up dis hombuggin' Debil's Mout' . . ."

Angrily, I said, "Timothy, Stew Cat is not a jumbi. You let him alone."

The old man was silent, and I was suddenly worried for Stew Cat's safety. Timothy stayed by me all night but in the morning, when I awakened, he was gone and so was Stew Cat.

I crawled out of the hut and began to call for Stew. Then I called for Timothy. There was no answer. I went down the hill and headed up the beach toward the reef. Voodoo was silly, I knew, but it was also frightening. I couldn't understand why Timothy thought Stew Cat was the jumbi.

I decided to circle the island to find them. Using my cane to feel the way, to touch driftwood or coral ledges the night tide might have uncovered, I moved along the damp sand, calling out now and then.

When I reached the north side, Timothy answered, "Marnin', Phill-eep."

I asked him where he'd been.

He laughed. "Dere is lil' place to go 'ere. I 'ave been 'ere on dis beach."

"Where is Stew Cat?"

Timothy was silent.

I asked again.

"B'gettin' his own self a lizzard, mebbe, mebbe," he answered, but there was something conniving in his voice.

All the while, I could hear a scraping noise and, occasionally, a ring of metal. "What are you doing?" I asked.

"Cuttin' on an ol' piece o' wood," he replied.

Why would he be down on north beach this early cutting wood? I knew we had plenty for the campfire and the signal fire.

"And you haven't seen Stew Cat?"

"Not a 'air," he said.

I wanted to see what he had in his hands, but I didn't have the courage to walk up and touch it. I said, "Timothy, I'm very hungry."

I felt his hand on my wrist. He said, "We'll go to d'hut."

He fixed breakfast, we ate, and then without a word, he slipped away.

Usually, he kept his hunting knife in the tin box that had stored our biscuits. Also in that box were the dry matches we had left, a few pieces of stale chocolate, and small things that Timothy had salvaged from the beach or the raft.

I felt a few nails, the hinges that had been on the raft's trap door, some short lengths of rope, a piece of cork, several small tin cans, and a small roll of something that felt like leather. Nothing was missing except the knife, and I knew he'd taken it to north beach with him.

As best I could, I searched around the hut area for Stew Cat, thinking maybe Timothy had tied him up somewhere. Yet I was certain he'd be meowing if he was within hearing distance.

I was positive that Timothy was back on north beach cutting on that piece of wood but something told me not to go down there. So I sat by the hut wondering what to do. It was no good trying to convince him that jumbi did not exist, nor was there any way to find Stew Cat if Timothy had hidden him.

The morning hours passed slowly. Once, I went down to east beach to sit near the signal fire, hoping to hear the drone of an aircraft. Several times, over the stir of the wind, I thought I heard a faint meow, but I couldn't locate the direction.

Maybe all that had happened was beginning to work on the old man's mind. Maybe I was stranded on a tiny, forgotten island in the Caribbean with a madman. If he harmed Stew Cat because of some silly jumbi thing, I knew he might also harm me.

I thought about getting back on the raft and letting it drift to sea again. I was certain that there were enough boards still on top to sit and sleep on. If I could get the water keg down the hill, and the last pieces of chocolate out of the box, I'd be all right for a few days.

I got up and went down to the water, feeling my way toward the reef. I knew that if I kept going that way, I'd touch or fall over the length of life-line rope that tethered the raft. Timothy had driven a heavy piece of driftwood into the sand so that the raft would not go out to sea with the tide.

I walked slowly and carefully, expecting at any moment to feel the rope with my cane, or have it hit against my ankles. I went all the way to the beginning of the reef without finding it. Then I reversed my course, and walked in the other direction. Finally, I stumbled over the heavy piece of wood that Timothy had driven into the sand.

I felt around it, but the rope was no longer tied to it. He'd cut the raft loose! Panic swept over me. But taking my bearing from the stake, I decided to go out into the water, hoping to find the raft.

A few feet offshore, I got another bad scare. I put my foot down and something moved. In fact the whole bottom seemed to move. I lost my balance and fell headfirst into the water. I came up sputtering, and realized I'd stepped on a skate, that diamond-shaped fish with a stinger tail. I'd done that once or twice at Westpunt. The skate is kin to the deadly sea ray, but this one was as shocked as I was and swam off to deep water.

I went out to my waist, feeling with my hands in all directions. But the raft was gone!

I trusted Timothy, and kept telling myself that he wouldn't harm me, but it was the whole mysterious jumbi thing that was frightening. And he certainly wasn't acting like the Timothy I'd been living with.

In midafternoon he returned to the hut. Neither of us spoke.

Then I heard him pounding something. The palm fronds on the hut rattled; whatever it was, he was pounding it into the hut. Having finished, he went away again.

When I heard him moving through the sea grape down the path, I got up and began feeling around the framing of the hut. There was nothing on the sides of it, and I decided that whatever he'd attached had to be on the roof.

I knew there were several lengths of log over near the campfire. So I approached it, found one of the logs, and rolled it over to the entrance to the hut. I stood on it and felt along the cross-frame that held the roof up.

In the very center I found what I was looking for. I cried out when the palm of my hand touched something sharp. Then with my fingers, I slowly felt around the object. It had a head, I discovered, four feet, and a tail.

Timothy had spent all that time carving a cat, a Stew Cat. The nails in it were supposed to kill the evil jumbi.

I felt weak and sat down on the log.

Soon, he came up the path, dropping Stew Cat into my lap.

"Where was he?" I asked.

"On d'raff, o' course," Timothy answered. "I got 'im off d'islan' till I could chase d'jumbi."

"Where is the raft, Timothy?"

"'Twas off d'shore, Phill-eep. 'Tis back now. An' our luck is change."

But it didn't change. It got worse.

CHAPTER

Twelve

ONE MORNING in the middle of May, I awakened to hear Timothy taking great breaths. It sounded as though he were fighting for air. I listened a moment and then asked, "Are you all right, Timothy?"

He wheezed back, "Feber! Malar!"

I had to think a moment to understand what he was talking about. Fever! Malaria! I reached over to touch him. His forehead was burning hot.

His breath coming in big, harsh sighs, he said,

"I got malar agin, Phill-eep. 'Twill go away, but fetch some wattah."

When I had had fever in Virginia, and at Scharloo, my mother had given me aspirin and then put cold cloths on my head. But we had no aspirin on the cay, of course, and the water was always warm. I poured some water from the keg, and gave it to him. He gulped it and then fell back on the mat.

For a while, I listened to his heavy breathing and then ripped a piece of cloth from what was left of my shirt, dampened it with water, and placed it on his forehead. He murmured, "Dat be good," but suddenly he began to shiver, even though the morning air was already warm. I could hear his teeth clacking.

I had nothing to cover him with, so I just sat beside him holding the cloth, which was already beginning to dry, to his forehead. His breath was like air from a furnace.

It must have been about ten o'clock when Timothy began to mumble and laugh. It sounded almost as if he were talking in his sleep, but the laughter, little bursts of it between the wheezes, was very high and strange. I couldn't keep the cloth on his head because he was tossing from side to side.

I talked to him constantly, but he didn't even seem to know I was there.

Once he got up but fell back down to the mat,

and I told him to stay very still. For a long time, he did, because he began to shiver again. When that ended, the mumbling and high laughter started all over.

At about noontime, the mumbling got worse, and I could feel him trying to get to his feet. I clung to his arm, shouting for him to lie down again, but he threw me aside as if I weren't there. I could hear him crashing down the hill toward the sea, the frightening laughter echoing back.

I followed the trail of laughter. Then I heard splashing and knew he'd gone into the water. I yelled, "Timothy, Timothy, come back."

Suddenly it became dead quiet. I screamed his name again and again. There was no answer.

I reached the beach and waded out to my knees, then began to move slowly along, trying to keep on a line with the beach. I had gone about thirty steps when I fell over Timothy's body, plunging down in the water.

Holding onto him with one hand, I got on my feet again. The upper part of his body was floating but I knew his feet were dragging on the bottom. I put my face against his mouth. Yes, he was still breathing.

I worked myself around to put both hands under his shoulders, but he was too heavy that way. Then I clasped my hands under his chin, and began to pull him out. He made strange sounds, but did not try to help me.

It took me what seemed like a long time to get Timothy out of the water and back up on the damp sand. He must have weighed two hundred and twenty or thirty pounds, and I could only move him two or three inches at a time.

I sat beside him for almost an hour in the hot sun while he rested quietly, his breathing not so harsh now. Then I realized he was shivering again. I knew I could not drag him up the slope to the shelter of the hut, so I tore off branches of sea grape and put them over his body. The grape leaves cut the rays of the sun.

I brought water down from the hut, raised his head, and ordered him to drink it. With one hand, I found his lips and then guided the cup to his chin. He seemed to understand and gulped it down.

I stayed by him the rest of the long afternoon while he slept. When he awakened, it was early evening and had turned cool again. He was breathing easily now, and I knew the fever had broken because his forehead was no longer hot.

Sitting up, he said weakly, "How did I get downg 'ere?"

I told him he'd run down the hill.

"Dat debil, d'fever," Timothy sighed.

I said, "You went into the water. You scared me, Timothy."

"Dat be true," he said. "My 'ead burn wid fire, an' I put it out."

I helped him to his feet, and we went up the hill together, Timothy leaning on me for support for the first time. He never really regained his strength.

CHAPTER

Thirteen

IT WAS IN LATE MAY that I believe Timothy decided we might stay there forever. We had not seen a schooner sail or heard an airplane since setting foot on the island.

I know it was late May because each day he dropped a small pebble into an old can that he'd found on the beach. It was our only way to tell how many days we'd been there. Every so often, I'd count them, beginning with April 9. We now had forty-eight pebbles in the can.

On this day, Timothy said thoughtfully, "Phill-eep, 'as it evah come into your own self that I might be poorly again some marnin'?" I knew he was thinking about malar and the fever.

I said it had.

He said, "Well, you mus' den know how to provite your own self wid feesh."

For more than a week, I knew he had been laboring over nails to turn them into fish hooks. He always speared the fish or langosta with a sharp stick, but I could not see, of course, to do that. I knew he was making the hooks for me.

He said, with a secret tone in his voice, "I 'ave foun' an outrageous good 'ole on d'reef in a safe place."

We went down the hill and started out along the reef shelf. By now, my feet were tough and I hardly felt the jagged edges of the coral. But I knew that lurking in the tide pools were the treacherous sea urchins. Stepping on them invited a sharp spine in your foot, and Timothy had already warned me that, "dey veree poison, dey b'gibbin' you terrible pain."

Every two feet, Timothy had driven a piece of driftwood deep into the coral crevices so that I could feel them as I went along. Neither of us knew what to do about the sea urchins but Timothy said he'd think mightily about them. He had taken a large rock to smash them all along the path over the reef top. But in time they would come back.

We went out about fifty feet along the reef, and then he said, "Now, we feesh."

He described the hole to me. It was about twenty feet in diameter and six to eight feet deep. The bottom was sandy, but mostly free of coral so that my hooks would not snag. He said there was a "mos'" natural opening to the sea, so that the fish could swim in and out of this coral-walled pool.

He took my hand to have me feel all around the edges of the hole. The coral had been smoothed over by centuries of sea wash. Timothy said that the sand in the sea water acted like a grindstone on the sharp edges of the coral. It was not completely smooth but there were no jagged edges sticking out.

"Now, reach downg 'ere," Timothy said, "an' tug off d'mussel."

I put my hand into the warm water, kneeling down over the ledge, and felt a mussel. But in ripping it loose, I lost my balance and only Timothy's hand prevented me from falling in. If you are blind, the sensation of falling can be terrifying. My memory of the fall off the raft was still very clear.

Timothy said, "Easy dere, Phill-eep. Jus' sit a moment an' relax."

His voice was soothing. "If evah you do fall, jus' stay in d'hole awhile, feel which way d'wattah washes, den follow it to d'ledge, grab hol', an' pull your own self out."

Timothy guided my hands in opening the tough

mussel shell and digging the slippery meat out to bait the hook. "'Tis an outrageous sharp knife, so be veree careful o' your fingers."

Then he told me to feel the hook and slip the mussel bait over the barb. I'd fished many times with my father and this was easy.

Rusty bolts served as sinkers. Timothy had found several pieces of wood with bolts in them; had burned them, then raked the bolts out of the ashes. He'd unraveled a life line from the raft to make single strands for the fishing line.

I dropped the hook and sinker overboard. In a moment, there was a sharp tug. I jerked, flipping the fish back over my shoulder so it would land on the reef. Timothy cheered and told me to feel along the line to the wriggling fish, then take the hook out.

Squirming and jumping in my hand, it was small but fat. I grinned over toward Timothy. When I had fished before, it was fun. Now, I felt I had done something very special. I was learning to do things all over again, by touch and feel.

I said to Timothy, "Dis is outrageous, hombuggin' good feesh 'ole."

He laughed with pleasure.

Every day after that I did all the fishing. Timothy, of course, continued to get langosta. He had to dive for them, but I caught all the fish. After the third morning, he let me go out alone on the reef. I'd feel my way along his driftwood stobs, find the hole, pry a mussel loose, and then fish.

I was alone on the reef but somehow I always felt he was sitting on the beach nearby. I could sense his presence, yet he was always at the hut when I got back there.

We often talked about the cay and what was on it. Timothy had not thought much about it. He took it for granted that the cay was always there, but I told him about geography, and how maybe a volcano could have caused the Devil's Mouth. He'd listen in fascination, almost speechless.

We talked about how the little coral animals might have been building the foundations of the cay for thousands of years. I said, "Then sand began to gather on it, and after more years, it was finally an island."

It was as if a new world had opened up for Timothy. He kept using that same expression, "Dat be true?"

I found out that he'd never thought about how the sea grape, or the vines, or the coconuts came to our cay. I told him what I knew.

Seeds had drifted in from the sea, or birds had brought them. After a rain, they'd taken root.

"D'lizzard?" he asked sternly.

"I'd bet a bird, flying from another island, holding a mother lizard in its beak, dropped it here. Then the baby lizards were born. Or maybe a mother lizard washed ashore on driftwood during a storm."

Timothy was very impressed, and I felt good that I'd been able to tell him something.

We found a lot to talk about.

I think it was the fifth afternoon of this week that I blurted out to Timothy, "I'll climb the palm now."

"Eh, Phill-eep," he said, and I could almost see the grin on his face and the light in his eyes as he looked skyward. Greedily, I'm sure.

He said, "Dere is one coconut tree ovah dere dat 'as a sway in 'is back like an ol' horse. Dat is d'one to clim'."

I was trembling a little as he led me to the tree, telling me I should go up just a short way; climb it like a monkey. If I could do it, I was to come back down, put the knife between my teeth, and go up again.

The trunk of this palm tree must have been about two feet in diameter because I could easily put my hands around to the back. I grasped it, hunched by body, placed my bare feet on the rough trunk, and began to climb. Timothy was probably holding his breath.

I went up about ten feet and froze. I could not move up or down. My legs and arms were rigid.

Timothy, standing below to catch me if I fell, called up softly, "Phill-eep, 'tis no shame to ease your own self back downg to d'san'."

Slowly I began to back down along the trunk.

The bark was rough against my hands and feet, but what I felt most was Timothy's disappointment. I couldn't have been more than a few feet off the ground when I took a deep breath and said to myself, If you fall, you'll fall in sand.

Then I started climbing again.

Timothy called up, "You 'ave forgot d'knife."

I knew that if I stopped now, I'd never climb it. I didn't answer him but kept my hands and feet moving steadily. Then I heard him shout, "You b'gettin' to d'top." Palm fronds brushed my head. I grasped the base of one to pull myself up. Timothy let out a roar of joy.

Then he told me how to reach the coconuts. It took a long time to pull, tug, and twist two of them loose. But they finally fell. I stayed in the palm another few minutes to rest, then slid down. I had won.

As my feet touched the ground, Timothy hugged me, yelling, "D'palm harass us no more."

We drank every drop of the coconut milk, and feasted on the fresh meat.

Squatting near me, his teeth crunching the coconut, Timothy said, "You see, Phill-eep, you do not need d'eye now. You 'ave done widout d'eye what I couldn't do wid my whole body."

It was almost as if I'd graduated from the survival course that Timothy had been putting me through since we had landed on the cay.

It rained that night, a very soft rain. Not even

enough to drip through the palm frond roof. Timothy breathed softly beside me. I had now been with him every moment of the day and night for two months, but I had not seen him. I remembered that ugly welted face. But now, in my memory, it did not seem ugly at all. It seemed only kind and strong.

I asked, "Timothy, are you still black?"

His laughter filled the hut.

CHAPTER

Fourteen

ONE VERY HOT MORNING in July, we were down on north beach where Timothy had found a patch of calico scallops not too far offshore. It was the hottest day we'd ever had on the cay. So hot that each breath felt like fire. And for once, the trade wind was not blowing. Nothing on the cay seemed to be moving.

North beach was a very strange beach anyway. The sand on it felt coarser to my feet. Everything about it felt different, but that didn't really make sense since it was only about a mile from south beach.

Timothy explained, "D'nawth is alles d'bleak beach on any islan'," but he couldn't say why.

He had just brought some calico scallops ashore when we heard the rifle shot. He came quickly to my side, saying, "Dat b'trouble."

Trouble? I thought it meant someone had found the cay. That wasn't trouble. Excited, I asked, "Who's shooting?"

"D'sea," he said.

I laughed at him, "The sea can't shoot a rifle."

"A crack like d'rifle," he said, worry in his voice. "It can make d'shot all right, all right. It b'tell us a veree bad starm is comin', Phill-eep. A tempis'."

I couldn't quite believe that. However, there had been, distinctly, a crack like a rifle or pistol shot.

He said anxiously, "D'waves do it. Somewhar far off, out beyond d'Grenadines, or in dat pesky bight off Honduras, a hurrican' is spawnin', young bahss. I feel it. What we heeard was a wave passin' dis lil' hombug point."

I heard him sniffing the air as if he could smell the hurricane coming. Without the wind, there was a breathless silence around our cay. The sea, he told me, was smooth as green jelly. But already, the water was getting cloudy. There were no birds in sight. The sky, he said, had a yellowish cast to it.

"Come along, we 'ave much to do. D'calico scallop can wait dey own self till after d'tempis'."

We went up to our hill.

Now I knew why he had chosen the highest point of land on the cay for our hut. Even so, I thought, the waves might tumble over it.

The first thing Timothy did was to lash our water keg high on a palm trunk. Next he took the remaining rope that we had and tied it securely around the same sturdy tree. "In case d'tempis' reach dis high, lock your arms ovah d'rope an' hang on, Phill-eep."

I realized then why he had used our rope sparingly; why he had made my guideline down to east beach from vines instead of rope. Everyday, I learned of something new that Timothy had done so we could survive.

During the afternoon, he told me this was a freak storm, because most did not come until September or October. August, sometimes. Seldom in July. "But dis year, d'sea be angry wid all d'death upon it. D'wahr."

The storms bred, Timothy said, in the eastern North Atlantic, south of the Cape Verde Islands, in the fall, but sometimes, when they were freaks, and early, they bred much closer, in a triangle way off the northeast tip of South America. Once in a great while, in June or July, they sometimes made up not far from Providencia and San Andrés. Near us. The June ones were only pesky, but the July ones were dangerous.

"Dis be a western starm, I b'guessin'. Dey out-rageous strong when dey come," he said.

Even Stew Cat was nervous. He was around my legs whenever I moved. I asked Timothy what we should do to protect him. He laughed. "Stew Cat b'go up d'palm on d'lee side iffen it b'gettin' too terrible. Don' worry 'bout Stew Cat."

Yet I could not help worrying. The thought of losing either of them was unbearable. If something bad happened on the cay, I wanted it to happen to all of us.

Nothing changed during the afternoon, although it seemed to get even hotter. Timothy spent a lot of time down at the raft, stripping off everything usable and carrying it back up the hill. He said we might never see it again, or else it might wash up the hill so that it would be impossible to launch.

Timothy was not purposely trying to frighten me about the violence of the storm; he was just being honest. He had good reason to be frightened him-self.

"In '28, I be on d'*Hettie Redd* sout' o' Antigua when d'tempis' hit. D'wind was outrageous, an' d'ol' schooner break up like chips fallin' 'fore d'ax. I wash ashore from d'sea, so wild no mahn believe it. No odder mahn from d'*Hettie Redd* live 'ceptin' me."

I knew that wild sea from long ago was much on Timothy's mind all afternoon.

We had a huge meal late in the day, much bigger than usual, because Timothy said we might not be able to eat for several days. We had fish and coconut meat, and we each drank several cups of coconut milk. Timothy said that the fish might not return to the reef for at least a week. He'd noticed that they'd already gone to deep water.

After we ate, Timothy carefully cleaned his knife and put it into the tin box, which he lashed high on the same tree that held our water keg.

"We ready, Phill-eep," he said.

CHAPTER

Fifteen

AT SUNSET, with the air heavy and hot, Timothy described the sky to me. He said it was flaming red and that there were thin veils of high clouds. It was so still over our cay that we could hear nothing but the rustling of the lizards.

Just before dark, Timothy said, "'Twon't be long now, Phill-eep."

We felt a light breeze that began to ripple the smooth sea. Timothy said he saw an arc of very black clouds to the west. They looked as though they were beginning to join the higher clouds.

I gathered Stew Cat close to me as we waited, feeling the warm breeze against my face. Now and then, there were gusts of wind that rattled the palm fronds, shaking the little hut.

It was well after dark when the first drops of rain spattered the hut, and with them, the wind turned cool. When it gusted, the rain hit the hut like handfuls of gravel.

Then the wind began to blow steadily, and Timothy went out of the hut to look up at the sky. He shouted, "Dey boilin' ovah now, Phill-eep. 'Tis hurrican', to be sure."

We could hear the surf beginning to crash as the wind drove waves before it, and Timothy ducked back inside to stand in the opening of the hut, his big body stretched so that he could hang onto the overhead frame, keeping the hut erect as long as possible.

I felt movement around my legs and feet. Things were slithering. I screamed to Timothy who shouted back, "B'nothin' but d'lil' lizzard, comin' high groun'."

Rain was now slashing into the hut, and the wind was reaching a steady howl. The crash of the surf sounded closer; I wondered if it was already beginning to push up toward our hill. The rain was icy, and I was wet, head to foot. I was shivering, but more from the thought of the sea rolling over us than from the sudden cold.

In a moment, there was a splintering sound, and Timothy dropped down beside me, covering my body with his. Our hut had blown away. He shouted, "Phill-eep, put your 'ead downg." I rolled over on my stomach, my cheek against the wet sand. Stew Cat burrowed down between us.

There was no sound now except the roar of the storm. Even the sound of the wind was being beaten down by the wildness of the sea. The rain was hitting my back like thousands of hard berries blown from air guns.

Once something solid hit us and then rolled on. "Sea grape," Timothy shouted. It was being torn up by the roots.

We stayed flat on the ground for almost two hours, taking the storm's punishment, barely able to breathe in the driving rain. Then Timothy shouted hoarsely, "To d'palm."

The sea was beginning to reach for our hilltop, climbing the forty feet with raging whitecaps. Timothy dragged me toward the palm. I held Stew Cat against my chest.

Standing with his back to the storm, Timothy put my arms through the loops of rope, and then roped himself, behind me, to the tree.

Soon, I felt water around my ankles. Then it washed to my knees. It would go back and then crash against us again. Timothy was taking the full blows of the storm, sheltering me with his body. When the water receded, it would tug at us, and

Timothy's strength would fight against it. I could feel the steel in his arms as the water tried to suck us away.

Even in front of him, crushed against the trunk of the palm, I could feel the rain, which was now jabbing into me like the punches of a nail. It was not falling toward earth but being driven straight ahead by the wind.

We must have been against the palm for almost an hour when suddenly the wind died down and the rain became gentle. Timothy panted, "D'eye! We can relax a bit till d'odder side o' d'tempis' hit us."

I remembered that hurricanes, which are great circling storms, have a calm eye in the center.

"Are you all right?" I asked.

He replied hoarsely, "I b'damp, but all right."

Yet I heard him making small noises, as if it were painful to move, as we stood back from the palm trunk. We sat down on the ground beside it, still being pelted with rain, to wait for the eye to pass. Water several inches deep swirled around us, but was not tugging at us.

It was strange and eerie in the eye of the hurricane. I knew we were surrounded on all sides by violent winds, but the little cay was calm and quiet. I reached over for Timothy. He was cradling his head in his arms, still making those small noises, like a hurt animal.

In twenty or thirty minutes, the wind picked up sharply and Timothy said that we must stand against the palm again. Almost within seconds, the full fury of the storm hit the cay once more. Timothy pressed me tightly against the rough bark.

It was even worse this time, but I do not remember everything that happened. We had been there awhile when a wave that must have reached halfway up the palms crashed against us. The water went way over my head. I choked and struggled. Then another giant wave struck us. I lost consciousness then. Timothy did, too, I think.

When I came to, the wind had died down, coming at us only in gusts. The water was still washing around our ankles, but seemed to be going back into the sea now. Timothy was still behind me, but he felt cold and limp. He was sagging, his head down on my shoulder.

"Timothy, wake up," I said.

He did not answer.

Using my shoulders, I tried to shake him, but the massive body did not move. I stood very still to see if he was breathing. I could feel his stomach moving and I reached over my shoulder to his mouth. There was air coming out. I knew that he was not dead.

However, Stew Cat was gone.

I worked for a few minutes to release my arms from the loops of rope around the palm trunk, and then slid out from under Timothy's body. He slumped lifelessly against the palm. I felt along the ropes that bound his forearms to the trunk until I found the knots.

With his weight against them, it was hard to pull them loose, even though they were sailor's knots and had loops in them. The rope was soaked, which made it worse.

I must have worked for half an hour before I had him free from the trunk. He fell backwards into the wet sand, and lay there moaning. I knew there was very little I could do for him except to sit by him in the light rain, holding his hand. In my world of darkness, I had learned that holding a hand could be like medicine.

After a long while, he seemed to recover. His first words, painful and dragged out, were, "Phill-eep . . . you . . . all right . . . be true?"

"I'm okay, Timothy," I said.

He said weakly, "Terrible tempis'."

He must have rolled over on his stomach in the sand, because his hand left mine abruptly. Then he went to sleep, I guess.

I touched his back. It felt warm and sticky. I ran my hand lightly down it, suddenly realizing that I, too, was completely naked. The wind and sea had torn our tatters of clothes from us.

Timothy had been cut to ribbons by the wind, which drove the rain and tiny grains of sand before it. It had flayed his back and his legs until there were very few places that weren't cut. He was bleeding, but there was nothing I could do to stop it. I found his hard, horny hand again, wrapped mine around it, and lay down beside him.

I went to sleep too.

Sometime long after dawn, I awakened. The rain had stopped, and the wind had died down to its usual whisper. But I think the clouds were still covering the sky because I could not feel the sun.

I said, "Timothy," but he did not answer me. His hand was cold and stiff in mine.

Old Timothy, of Charlotte Amalie, was dead.

I stayed there beside him for a long time, very tired, thinking that he should have taken me with him wherever he had gone. I did not cry then. There are times when you are beyond tears.

I went back to sleep, and this time when I awakened, I heard a meow. Then I cried for a long time, holding Stew Cat tight. Aside from him, I was blind and alone on a forgotten cay.

CHAPTER
Sixteen

IN THE AFTERNOON, I groped west along the hill. Thirty or forty feet from the last palm tree, I began to dig a grave for Timothy. I cleared palm fronds, chunks of sea grape, pieces of wood, dead fish, fan coral, and shells that the sea had thrown up. I marked out a space about seven feet long and four feet wide. Then I dug with my hands.

At first I was angry with Timothy. I said to Stew Cat, "Why did he leave us alone here?" Then as I dug, I had other thoughts.

With his great back to the storm, taking its full punishment, he had made it possible for me to live. When my grandfather died, my father had said, "Phillip, sometimes people die from just being very, very tired." I think that is what happened to Timothy.

I also think that had I been able to see, I might not have been able to accept it all. But strangely, the darkness separated me from everything. It was as if my blindness were protecting me from fear.

I buried Timothy, placing stones at the head of the grave to mark it. I didn't know what to say over the grave. I said, "Thank you, Timothy," and then turned my face to the sky. I said, "Take care of him, God, he was good to me."

There didn't seem to be anything else to say, so I just stood by his grave for a while. Then I felt my way back to the spot where our hut had been. I located wood and piled it around the base of the palm tree that held our water keg and the tin box. Both were to the lee side of the storm.

It took me a long time to get the keg and the tin box to the ground, but I found, on opening the bung, that the water was still sweet and that the matches, wrapped in cellophane inside the tin box, were dry. But the two small bars of chocolate that we had been saving for a "feast," were ruined. I had no taste for them, anyway.

Feeling it everywhere under my feet, I knew that the cay was littered with debris. I started cleaning

the camp area, or what was left of it. I piled all
the palm fronds, frayed by the wind, in one place;
sticks of wet driftwood in another.

With Stew Cat constantly around—I stumbled
over him several times—I worked until I felt it was
nearing darkness. I'd found one lone coconut in a
mass of sea grape and broken sticks. I opened it
and ate the meat, offering to share with Stew Cat,
who didn't seem interested.

Then I made a bed of palm fronds and sprawled
out on it, listening to the still angry sea as it tumbled
around the damp cay and thinking: I must feed
myself and Stew Cat; I must rebuild the hut and
build another signal fire down on east beach; then
I must spend each day listening for the sound of
aircraft. I knew Timothy had already given up on
any schooner entering the dangerous Devil's Mouth.

I was certain that the sea had washed away Timothy's markers atop the coral reef, and I was also
sure that my guide vine-rope leading down to the
beach had been snapped and tangled by the storm.

But now, for the first time, I fully understood
why Timothy had so carefully trained me to move
around the island, and the reef . . .

The reef, I thought.

How could I fish without any poles? They must
have been washed away. Then I remembered Timothy saying that he would put them in a safe place.
The trouble was he'd forgotten to tell me where.

I got up and began to run my hands over each

palm trunk. On one of them I touched rope. I
followed it around to the lee side with my fingers.
And there they were! Not two or three, but at
least a dozen, lashed together, each with a barbed
hook and bolt sinker. They were one more part of
the legacy Timothy had left me.

The sun came out strong in the morning. I could
feel it on my face. It began to dry the island,
and toward noon, I heard the first cry of a bird.
They were returning.

By now, I had taught myself to tell time, very
roughly, simply by turning my head toward the
direct warmth of the sun. If the angle was almost
overhead, I knew it was around noon. If it was
low, then of course, it was early morning or late
evening.

There was so much to do that I hardly knew
where to start. Get a campfire going, pile new wood
for a signal fire, make another rain catchment for
the water keg, weave a mat of palm fibers to sleep
on. Then make a shelter of some kind, fish the
hole on the reef, inspect the palm trees to see if
any coconuts were left—I didn't think any could be
up there—and search the whole island to discover
what the storm had deposited. It was enough work
for weeks, and I said to Stew Cat, "I don't know
how we'll get it all done." But something told me
I must stay very busy and not think about myself.

I accomplished a lot in three days, even putting

a new edge on Timothy's knife by honing it on coral. I jabbed it into the palm nearest my new shelter, so that I would always know where it was if I needed it. Without Timothy's eyes, I was finding that in my world, everything had to be very precise; an exact place for everything.

On the fifth day after the storm, I began to scour the island to find out what had been cast up. It was exciting, and I knew it would take days or weeks to accomplish. I had made another cane, and beginning with east beach, I felt my way back and forth, reaching down to touch everything that my cane struck; sometimes having to spend a long time trying to decide what it was that I held in my hands.

I found several large cans and used one of them to start the "time" can again, dropping five pebbles into it so that the reckoning would begin again from the night of the storm. I discovered an old broom, and a small wooden crate that would make a nice stool. I found a piece of canvas, and tried to think of ways to make pants from it, but I had no needle or thread.

Other than that, I found many shells, some bodies of dead birds, pieces of cork, and chunks of sponge, but nothing I could really put to good use.

It was on the sixth day after the storm, when I was exploring on south beach, that I heard the birds. Stew Cat was with me, as usual, and he growled when they first screeched. Their cries were angry, and I guessed that seven or eight might be in the air.

I stood listening to them; wondering what they were. Then I felt a beat of wing past my face, and an angry cry as the bird dived at me. I lashed out at it with my cane, wondering why they were attacking me.

Another dived down, screaming at me, and his bill nipped the side of my head. For a moment, I was confused, not knowing whether to run for cover under sea grape, or what was left of it, or try to fight them off with my cane. There seemed to be a lot of birds.

Then one pecked my forehead sharply, near my eyes, and I felt blood run down my face. I started to walk back toward camp, but had taken no more than three or four steps when I tripped over a log. I fell into the sand, and at the same time, felt a sharp pain in the back of my head. I heard a raging screech as the bird soared up again. Then another bird dived at me.

I heard Stew Cat snarling and felt him leap up on my back, his claws digging into my flesh. There was another wild screech, and Stew Cat left my back, leaping into the air.

His snarls and the wounded screams of the bird filled the stillness over the cay. I could hear them battling in the sand. Then I heard the death caw of the bird.

I lay still a moment. Finally, I crawled to where

Stew Cat had his victim. I touched him; his body was rigid and his hair was still on edge. He was growling, low and muted.

Then I touched the bird. It had sounded large, but it was actually rather small. I felt the beak; it was very sharp.

Slowly, Stew Cat began to relax.

Wondering what had caused the birds to attack me, I felt around in the sand. Soon, my hand touched a warm shell. I couldn't blame the birds very much. I'd accidently walked into their new nesting ground.

They were fighting for survival, after the storm, just as I was. I left Stew Cat to his unexpected meal and made my way slowly back to camp.

CHAPTER

Seventeen

TEN PEBBLES had gone into my "time" can when
I decided to do something Timothy had told me
never to do. I was tired of eating fish and sea-
grape leaves, and I wanted to save the few green
coconuts I'd managed to find on the ground. There
were none left in the trees.

I wanted scallops or a langosta to roast over the
fire. I didn't dare go out off north beach for scallops
because of the sharks. But I thought there might

be a langosta clinging to coral at the bottom of the fishing hole.

From what Timothy had told me, the sea entrance to the hole was too narrow for a large fish, a shark, to swim through. Barracuda, he'd said, could go through, but they were not usually dangerous. If there happened to be an octopus down there, it would have to be a very small one. The big ones were always in deep water. So he'd said it was safe for him to dive in the hole.

I sharpened a stick the way Timothy had done, but I knew that if I felt a langosta with my left hand, I would have to be very quick with my right hand, or he would use his tail to push away from me across the sand.

With Stew Cat, I went down to the reef and felt my way along it until I found the familiar edges of the hole. I told Stew Cat, "If I'm not out in twenty minutes, you better jump in and get me."

The crazy cat rubbed along my leg and purred.

Holding the sharpened stick in my right hand, I slipped into the warm water, treading for a moment, waiting to see if anything came up. Then I ducked my head underwater, swam down a few feet, and came up again. I was certain that nothing was in the hole aside from the usual small fish I yanked out each morning.

After a few minutes, I had my courage up and dived to the bottom, holding the sharp stick in

my left hand now, and using my right hand to feel
the coral and rocks. Coming up now and then for
air, I slowly felt my way around the bottom of the
small pool, touching sea fans that waved back and
forth, feeling the organ-pipe coral and the bigger
chunks of brain coral.

Several times I was startled when seaweed or sea
fans would brush against my face and swam quickly
to the surface. It must have taken me nearly thirty
minutes to decide that I could hunt langosta in the
hole.

This time, I dived in earnest. I went straight
down, touched the bottom, and then took a few
strokes toward the coral sides of the pool. Timothy
had said that langosta were always on the bottom,
usually over against the rocks and coral. To my
amazement, I touched one on the first sweep and
drove the sharp stick into him, swimming quickly
to the surface.

Panting, I shouted to Stew Cat, "Lobster tonight!"

I swam to the edge, pushed the langosta off
the stick, caught my breath again, and dived.

I dived many times without again touching the
hard shell that meant langosta. I began sticking my
hands deeper into the shelves and over the ledges
near the bottom.

I rested a few minutes, then decided I'd make
one more dive. I was happy with the lobster that

The concept

was now on the reef, but it was quite small, barely a meal for Stew Cat and myself.

I dived again, and this time found what seemed to be an opening into a deep hole. Or at least, the hole went far back. There has to be a big lobster in there, I thought. Up I came again, filled my lungs, and dived immediately.

I ran my hand back into the hole, and something grabbed it.

Terrified, I put my feet against the rocks to pull away. The pain was severe. Whatever had my wrist had the strength of Timothy's arms. I jerked hard and whatever it was came out with my arm, its tail smashing against my chest. I kicked and rose to the surface, the thing still on my wrist, its teeth sunk in deep.

I'm sure I screamed as I broke water, flailing toward the edge of the hole. Then the thing let loose, and I made it up over the side and out of the hole.

Pain shooting up my entire arm, I lay panting on the edge of the pool and gingerly began to feel my wrist. It was bleeding, but not badly. But the teeth had sunk in deep.

It wasn't a fish, because the body felt long and narrow. Some time later, I made an informed guess that it had been a large moray eel. Whatever it was, I never got back into the hole again.

CHAPTER

Eighteen

THERE WAS NO DAY or night that passed when I didn't listen for sounds from the sky. Both my sense of touch and my sense of hearing were beginning to make up for my lack of sight. I separated the sounds and each became different.

I grew to know the different cries of the birds that flew by the cay, even though I had no idea what any of them were. I made up my own names for them according to the sound of their cries. Only the occasional bleat of the gull gave me a picture of that bird, for I had heard and seen them many times around the sea wall in Willemstad.

I knew how the breeze sounded when it crossed the sea grape. It fluttered the small leaves. When it went through the palm fronds the storm hadn't ripped away, it made a flapping noise.

I knew the rustle of the lizards. Some were still on the island after the storm. I could only guess they'd somehow climbed high into the palms. Otherwise, how could they have lived with water lapping over the entire cay?

I even knew when Stew Cat was approaching me. His soft paws on a dried leaf made only a tiny crackle, but I heard it.

One midmorning in early August, I was on the hill, near the camp, when I heard the far-off drone of an airplane. It was up-wind from me, but the sound was very clear. I reached down to feel Stew Cat. He had heard it too. His body was tense; his head pointed toward the sound.

I dropped to my knees by the fire, feeling around the edges until I grasped the end of a stick. I drew it back. Timothy had taught me to lay the fire sticks like a wheel, so that the fire burned slowly in the center, but always had a few un- burned ends on the outside. I tended the fire a half dozen times each day.

I spit on the stick until I heard a sizzle. Then I knew there was enough fire or charring on it to

light off the base of fried palm fronds beneath
the signal fire.

I listened again for the drone. Yes, it was still
there. Closer now.

I ran down the hill straight to the signal fire,
felt around the palm fronds, and then pushed the
stick over them. I blew on it until I heard the
crackle of flames. In a few minutes the signal fire
was roaring, and I ran to south beach where I
would be able to hear the aircraft without hearing
the crackling fire.

Standing on south beach, I listened. The plane
was coming closer!

I yelled toward the sky, "Here! Down here!"

I decided to run back to east beach to stand
near the fire and the new arrangement of rocks that
spelled out "Help."

Thinking any moment the plane would dive and
I would hear the roar of its engines across the cay
at low altitude, I stood with Stew Cat a few feet
from the sloshing surf. I waited and waited, but
there was no thundering sound from the sky. I
could hear nothing but the crackling of the fire, the
washing sound of the surf.

I ran back to south beach, where I stood very
still and listened.

The plane had gone!

Slowly, I returned to east beach and sat down
in sea-grape shade. I put my head down on my

arms and sobbed, feeling no shame for what I was
doing.

There seemed to be no hope of ever leaving the
cay, yet I knew I could not always live this way.
One day I would become ill or another storm would
rage against the island. I could never survive alone.

There had been many bad and lonely days and
nights, but none as bad as this.

Stew Cat came up, purring, rubbing along my
legs. I held him a long time, wondering why the
aircraft had not come down when the pilots saw
the smoke.

At last I thought, perhaps they didn't see the
smoke. I knew it was going up into the sky, but
was it white smoke that might be lost in the blue-
white sky, or was it dark and oily smoke that would
make a smudge against the blueness? There was no
way to tell.

If only there were some oily boards! The kind
that drifted around the waters of the Schottegat.
But I knew that the wood floating up on the beach
consisted mostly of branches or stumps that had
been in the water for weeks or months. There was
nothing in them to make dark smoke.

I began to think of all the things on the island.
Green palm fronds might send off dark smoke, but
until they were dried, they were too tough to tear
off the trees. The vines on north beach might make
dark smoke, but the leaves on them were very
small.

The sea grape! I snapped some off, feeling it between my fingers. Yes, there was oil in it. I got up and went over to the fire, tossing a piece in. In a moment, I heard it popping the way hot grease pops when it is dropped into water.

I knew how to do it now.

The smoke would rise from the cay in a fat, black column to lead the planes up the Devil's Mouth. If I heard another aircraft, I'd start a fire and then throw bundles of sea grape into it until I was certain a strong signal was going up from the island.

Timothy hadn't thought about black smoke, I was sure. That was it!

Feeling better now, I walked back up the hill to gather the few palm fronds that were left for a new fire base.

I woke up at dawn on the morning of August 20, 1942, to hear thunder and wondered when the first drops of rain would spatter on the roof of the shelter. I heard Stew Cat, down near my feet, let off a low growl.

I said, "It's only thunder, Stew Cat. We need the water."

But as I continued to listen, it did not seem to be thunder. It was a heavy sound, hard and sharp, not rolling. More like an explosion or a series of explosions. It felt as if the cay were shaking. I got up from the mat, moving out from under the shelter.

The air did not feel like rain. It was dry and there was no heavy heat.

"They're explosions, Stew," I said. "Very near us."

Maybe destroyers, I thought. I could not hear any aircraft engines. Maybe destroyers fighting it out with enemy submarines. And those heavy, hard, sharp sounds could be the depth charges that my father said were used by the Navy to sink U-boats.

This time, I didn't bother to take a piece of firewood down to east beach. I dug into the tin box for the cellophane wrapped package of big wooden matches. Four were left. I ran down the hill.

At the signal fire, I searched around for a rock. Finding one, I knelt down by the fire and struck a match against it. Nothing happened. I felt the head of the match. The sulphur had rubbed off. I struck another. It made a small popping noise and then went out.

I had two more matches left, and for a moment, I didn't know whether to use them or run back up the hill to the campfire.

I stopped to listen, feeling sweat trickle down my face. The explosions were still thundering across the sea.

Then I heard the drone of an aircraft. I took a deep breath and struck the next to last match. I heard it flare and ran my left hand over the top of it. There was heat. It was burning.

I reached deep into the fire pile, holding the match there until it began to burn the tips of my fingers. The fire caught and in a moment was roaring.

I ran across the beach to begin pulling sea grape down. I carried the first bundle to the fire and threw it in. Soon, I could smell it burning. It began to pop and crackle as the flames got to the natural oils in the branches.

By the time I had carried ten or fifteen bundles of sea grape to the fire, tumbling them in, I was sure that a column of black smoke was rising into the sky over the cay.

Suddenly, a deafening roar swept overhead. I knew it was an aircraft crossing the cay not much higher than the palms. I could feel the wind from it.

Forgetting for a moment, I yelled, "Timothy, they've come."

The aircraft seemed to be making a sharp turn. It roared across the cay again, seeming even lower this time because the rush of wind from it was hot. I could smell exhaust fumes.

I yelled, "Down here, down here," and waved my arms.

The plane made another tight circle, coming back almost directly over me. Its engine was screaming.

I shouted at Stew Cat, "We'll be rescued!" But

I think that he'd gone to hide in the sea grape.

This time, however, the aircraft did not circle back. It did not make another low pass over the island. I heard the sound going away. Soon, it had vanished completely. Then I realized that the explosions had stopped too.

A familiar silence settled over the cay.

All the strength went out of my body. It was the first real chance of rescue, and maybe there would not be another. The pilot had flown away, perhaps thinking I was just another native fisherman waving at an aircraft. I knew that the color of my skin was very dark now.

Worse, I knew that the smoke might have blotted out the lines of rocks that spelled help.

Feeling very ill, I climbed the slope again, throwing myself down on the mat in the hut. I didn't cry. There was no use in doing that.

I wanted to die.

After a while, I looked over toward Timothy's grave. I said, "Why didn't you take us with you?"

CHAPTER

Nineteen

IT WAS ABOUT NOON when I heard the bell.

It sounded like bells I'd heard in St. Anna Bay and in the Schottegat. Small boats and tugs use them to tell the engineer to go slow or fast or put the engines in reverse.

For a moment, I thought I was dreaming.

Then I heard the bell again. And with it, the slow chugging of an engine. And voices! They were coming from east beach.

I ran down there. Yes, a small boat had come into the Devil's Mouth and was approaching our cay.

I yelled, "I'm here! I'm here!"

There was a shout from across the water. A man's voice. "We see you!"

I stood there on east beach, Stew Cat by my feet, looking in the direction of the sounds. I heard the bell again; then the engine went into reverse, the propeller thrashing. Someone yelled, "Jump, Scotty, the water's shallow."

The voice was American, I was certain.

The engine was now idling, and someone was coming toward me. I could hear him padding across the sand. I said, "Hello."

There was no answer from the man. I suppose he was just staring at me.

Then he yelled to someone on the boat, "My Lord, it's a naked boy. And a cat!"

The person on the boat yelled, "Anyone else?"

I called out, "No, just us."

I began to move toward the man on the beach. He gasped. "Are you blind?"

I said, "Yes, sir."

In a funny voice, he asked, "Are you all right?"

"I'm fine now. You're here," I said.

He said, "Here, boy, I'll help you."

I said, "If you'll carry Stew Cat, you can just lead me to the boat."

After I had climbed aboard, I remembered Timothy's knife stuck in the palm tree. It was the only thing I wanted off the cay. The sailor who had carried Stew Cat went up the hill to get it while the other sailor asked me questions. When the first sailor came back from the hill, he said, "You wouldn't believe what's up there." I guess he was talking about our hut and the rain catchment. He should have seen the ones Timothy built.

I don't remember everything that happened in the next few hours but very soon I was helped up the gangway of a destroyer. On deck I was asked so many questions all at once that one man barked, "Stop badgering him. Give him food, medical care, and get him into a bunk."

A voice answered meekly, "Yes, sir, Cap'n."

Down in sick bay, the captain asked, "What's your name, son?"

"Phillip Enright. My father lives in Willemstad. He works for Royal Dutch Shell," I answered.

The captain told someone to get a priority radio message off to the naval commander at Willemstad and then asked, "How did you get on that little island?"

"Timothy and I drifted on to it after the *Hato* was sunk."

"Where's Timothy?" he asked.

I told the captain about Timothy and what had happened to us. I'm not sure the captain believed any of it, because he said quietly, "Son, get some sleep. The *Hato* was sunk way back in April."

I said, "Yes, sir, that's right," and then a doctor came in to check me over.

That night, after the ship had been in communication with Willemstad, the captain visited me again to tell me that his destroyer had been hunting a German submarine when the plane had spotted my black smoke and radioed back to the ship.

There was still disbelief in his voice when he said he'd checked all the charts and publications on the bridge; our cay was so small that the charts wouldn't even dignify it with a name. But Timothy had been right. It was tucked back up in the Devil's Mouth.

The next morning, we docked at the naval base in Cristóbal, Panama, and I was rushed to a hospital, although I really didn't think it was necessary. I was strong and healthy, the doctor on the destroyer had said.

My mother and father flew over from Willemstad in a special plane. It was minutes before they could say anything. They just held me, and I knew my mother was crying. She kept saying, "Phillip, I'm sorry, I'm so sorry."

The Navy had notified them that I was blind, so that it would not be a shock. And I knew I looked different. They'd brought a barber in to cut my hair, which had grown quite long.

We talked for a long time, Stew Cat on my bed, and I tried to tell them all about Timothy and the cay. But it was very difficult. They listened, of course, but I had the feeling that neither of them really understood what had happened on our cay.

Four months later, in a hospital in New York, after many X rays and tests, I had the first of three operations. The piece of timber that had hit me the night the *Hato* went down had damaged some nerves. But after the third operation, when the bandages came off, I could see again. I would always have to wear glasses, but I could see. That was the important thing.

In early April, I returned to Willemstad with my mother, and we took up life where it had been left off the previous April. After I'd been officially reported lost at sea, she'd gone back to Curaçao to be with my father. She had changed in many ways. She had no thoughts of leaving the islands now.

I saw Henrik van Boven occasionally, but it wasn't the same as when we'd played the Dutch or the British. He seemed very young. So I spent a lot of time along St. Anna Bay, and at the Ruyterkade market talking to the black people. I liked the sound of their voices. Some of them had known old Timothy from Charlotte Amalie. I felt close to them.

At war's end, we moved away from Scharloo and Curaçao. My father's work was finished.

Since then, I've spent many hours looking at charts of the Caribbean. I've found Roncador, Rosalind, Quito Sueño, and Serranilla Banks; I've found Beacon Cay and North Cay, and the islands of

Providencia and San Andrés. I've also found the Devil's Mouth.

Someday, I'll charter a schooner out of Panama and explore the Devil's Mouth. I hope to find the lonely little island where Timothy is buried.

Maybe I won't know it by sight, but when I go ashore and close my eyes, I'll know this was our own cay. I'll walk along east beach and out to the reef. I'll go up the hill to the row of palm trees and stand by his grave.

I'll say, "Dis b'dat outrageous cay, eh, Timothy?"

CONNECTIONS

Unlike Philip, this survivor is alone. She is out of food and lost in a frozen, barren region—the tundra of northern Alaska. In this part of the novel Julie of the Wolves, *she realizes that her life depends on a very unusual source. Making contact could be dangerous.*

Lost on the Tundra
from Julie of the Wolves
Jean Craighead George

Miyax pushed back the hood of her sealskin parka and looked at the Arctic sun. It was a yellow disc in a lime-green sky, the colors of six o'clock in the evening and the time when the wolves awoke. Quietly she put down her cooking pot and crept to the top of a dome-shaped frost heave, one of the many earth buckles that rise and fall in the crackling cold of the Arctic winter. Lying on her stomach, she looked across a vast lawn of grass and moss and focused her attention on the wolves she had come upon two sleeps ago. They were wagging their tails as they awoke and saw each other.

Her hands trembled and her heartbeat quickened, for she was frightened, not so much of the wolves, who were shy and many harpoon-shots away, but because of her desperate predicament. Miyax was lost. She had been lost without food for many sleeps on the North Slope of Alaska. The barren slope stretches for three hundred miles from the Brooks Range to the Arctic Ocean, and for more than eight hundred miles from the Chukchi to the Beaufort Sea. No roads cross it; ponds and lakes freckle its immensity. Winds scream across it, and the view in every direction is exactly the same. Somewhere in this cosmos was Miyax; and the very life in her body, its spark and warmth, depended upon these wolves for survival. And she was not so sure they would help.

Miyax stared hard at the regal black wolf, hoping to catch his eye. She must somehow tell him that she was starving and ask him for food. This could be done she knew, for her father, an Eskimo hunter, had done so. One year he had camped near a wolf den while on a hunt. When a month had passed and her father had seen no game, he told the leader of the wolves that he was hungry and needed food. The next night the wolf called him from far away and her father went to him and found a freshly killed caribou. Unfortunately, Miyax's father never explained to her how he had told the wolf of his needs. And not long afterward he paddled his kayak into the Bering Sea to hunt for seal, and he never returned.

She had been watching the wolves for two days, trying to discern which of their sounds and movements expressed goodwill and friendship. Most animals had such signals. The little Arctic ground squirrels flicked their tails sideways to notify others of their kind that they were friendly. By imitating this signal with her forefinger, Miyax had lured many a squirrel to her hand. If she could discover such a gesture for the wolves she would be able to make friends with them and share their food, like a bird or a fox.

Propped on her elbows with her chin in her fists, she stared at the black wolf, trying to catch his eye. She had chosen him because he was much larger than the others, and because he walked like her father, Kapugen, with his head high and his chest out. The black wolf also possessed wisdom, she had observed. The pack looked to him when the wind carried strange scents or the birds cried nervously. If he was alarmed, they were alarmed. If he was calm, they were calm.

Long minutes passed, and the black wolf did not look at

her. He had ignored her since she first came upon them, two sleeps ago. True, she moved slowly and quietly, so as not to alarm him; yet she did wish he would see the kindness in her eyes. Many animals could tell the difference between hostile hunters and friendly people by merely looking at them. But the big black wolf would not even glance her way.

A bird stretched in the grass. The wolf looked at it. A flower twisted in the wind. He glanced at that. Then the breeze rippled the wolverine ruff on Miyax's parka and it glistened in the light. He did not look at that. She waited. Patience with the ways of nature had been instilled in her by her father. And so she knew better than to move or shout. Yet she must get food or die. Her hands shook slightly and she swallowed hard to keep calm. . . .

Amaroq glanced at his paw and slowly turned his head her way without lifting his eyes. He licked his shoulder. A few matted hairs sprang apart and twinkled individually. Then his eyes sped to each of the three adult wolves that made up his pack and finally to the five pups who were sleeping in a fuzzy mass near the den entrance. The great wolf's eyes softened at the sight of the little wolves, then quickly hardened into brittle yellow jewels as he scanned the flat tundra.

Not a tree grew anywhere to break the monotony of the gold-green plain, for the soils of the tundra are permanently frozen. Only moss, grass, lichens, and a few hardy flowers take root in the thin upper layer that thaws briefly in summer. Nor do many species of animals live in this rigorous land, but those creatures that do dwell here exist in bountiful numbers. Amaroq watched a large cloud of Lapland longspurs wheel up into the sky, then alight in the grasses. Swarms of crane flies, one of the few insects that can survive the cold, darkened the tips of the mosses. Birds wheeled, turned, and called. Thousands sprang up from the ground like leaves in a wind.

The wolf's ears cupped forward and tuned in on some distant message from the tundra. Miyax tensed and listened, too. Did he hear some brewing storm, some approaching enemy? Apparently not. His ears relaxed and he rolled to his side. She sighed, glanced at the vaulting sky, and was painfully aware of her predicament.

Here she was, watching wolves—she, Miyax, daughter of Kapugen, adopted child of Martha, citizen of the United States, pupil at the Bureau of Indian Affairs School in Barrow, Alaska, and thirteen-year-old wife of the boy Daniel. She shivered at the thought of Daniel, for it was he who had driven her to this fate. She had run away from him exactly seven sleeps ago, and because of this she had one more title by gussak standards— the child divorcée.

The wolf rolled to his belly.

"Amaroq," she whispered. "I am lost and the sun will not set for a month. There is no North Star to guide me."

Amaroq did not stir.

"And there are no berry bushes here to bend under the polar wind and point to the south. Nor are there any birds I can follow." She looked up. "Here the birds are buntings and long- spurs. They do not fly to the sea twice a day like the puffins and sandpipers that my father followed."

The wolf groomed his chest with his tongue.

"I never dreamed I could get lost, Amaroq," she went on, talking out loud to ease her fear. "At home on Nunivak Island where I was born, the plants and birds pointed the way for wanderers. I thought they did so everywhere . . . and so, great black Amaroq, I'm without a compass."

It had been a frightening moment when two days ago she realized that the tundra was an ocean of grass on which she was circling around and around. Now as that fear overcame her again she closed her eyes. When she opened them her heart skipped excitedly. Amaroq was looking at her!

■ ■ ■

How long would Phillip have survived if Timothy hadn't been with him? In Far North, *teenagers Gabe Rogers and Raymond Providence discuss a similar question. They are stranded in the Canadian wilderness, and winter is coming. Fortunately, they are not alone: Johnny Raven, Raymond's great-uncle, is stranded with them. Would the boys really be "dead meat" without him? Read on—and judge for yourself.*

Without Him We're Dead Meat

from Far North

Will Hobbs

The old man stood on the top of the bank, taking the measure of Deadmen Valley, watching the cold wind bend the trees down. He was scanning the high mountains that had us encircled. What was he thinking? Were we going to stay here now? Our remaining moose meat couldn't have weighed twenty-five pounds. But Johnny had those three bullets. Our lives were in his hands now.

A quick fire and dry clothes, a lean-to and a night's supply of firewood, then darkness. A little dried fruit to eat and the howling of wolves across the river. I was utterly exhausted, and I had a deep ache in my side, pain whenever I breathed or moved. Had I recracked the rib? "Wolves in the valley should mean moose," Raymond grunted in my direction.

Johnny Raven was looking into the fire as he warmed his hands and feet. He seemed to be letting his mind drift, and I couldn't blame him. How did he keep going? For such a gentle man he was tough as nails.

"This bare ground will make tough moose hunting," Raymond said, holding out his hands to the fire and stamping his feet. "I wish it would snow about four or five feet—that's when the moose stick to just a few trails so they can get around. Sometimes they stand right in our snowmobile trails—won't even get out of the way."

"I can't believe we're hoping for snow, but I see what you mean. Could we even get around?"

"We've got the moose hide. Johnny can make snowshoes now. Tomorrow, I bet he finds some birch and starts making the frames."

"Without him . . ." I didn't want to finish my thought.

Raymond finished it for me: "Without him we're dead meat."

The old man stood up. By the light of the fire, he started stowing what was left of our moose meat in one of the army boxes. Then he picked up the rifle, motioned for us to follow him, and started to walk away. I was confused, and so was Raymond. Where did he want us to go? I wasn't about to force an explanation from him, that was for sure. I thought of grabbing the flashlight, then remembered it was dead. As the crescent moon disappeared behind the mountains towering over the valley, we walked into the darkness, following his silhouette.

Beyond the firelight the stars were blazing in the brittle, dry air. Even with only a few patches of crusted snow here and there to reflect the starlight, my eyes adjusted and I could make out where I was going. We followed the old man upriver as, from nowhere and everywhere, curtains of iridescent green and yellow light materialized in the night sky, swirling and shimmering and dancing. The northern lights. My father had often told me about them, the aurora borealis. I stopped to stare at the dazzling aurora shifting in a moment from horizon to horizon, returning just as fast, this time like brilliant searchlights. I ran to catch up, and then I walked with my eyes on the eerie lights and their strange, shifting shapes.

Where a small creek, almost frozen shut, reached the Nahanni, the old man turned away from the river and led us into the big trees. Then he pointed, and we could make out a small cabin in a clearing up ahead. The cabin was glowing yellow-green under the light of the aurora, and it looked like an apparition. Nearby stood a food cache on tall stilts. "Patterson," the old man said, pointing at the cabin.

"Johnny knew about this place!" Raymond exclaimed. "He must have been here before."

Johnny Raven fashioned a torch from a rolled piece of birchbark. By its light we lifted the cabin's latch and swung the door open on creaking hinges. We stepped over the doorsill, which was the shaved top of the second log up from the ground. The torchlight fell on a small woodstove in the corner and sections of stovepipe lying on the dirt floor. About thirteen feet square and tall enough for us to stand even in the corners, the cabin had a couple of shelves and a crude hand-made table—that was all there was to it. Above the table, the initials *RMP* and GM were carved large on the logs, along with the inscription *Deadmen Valley 1927*. The old man pointed at the initials and repeated that name, "Patterson."

"A trapper?" Raymond muttered to his great-uncle, and the old man nodded his agreement.

"You knew him?" Raymond asked. He pointed at the name, and then looked back to the old man. "You knew him?"

Johnny was nodding vigorously.

We returned to our campfire for the night. Raymond and I stayed up close to the fire as Johnny wrapped himself in his blanket, lay down, and slept. "At least we have a cabin to stay in now," I said. "A cabin with a stove—we can stay warm. Do you think that plane will come back, take a look around here?"

"We should get a signal fire going in case it does," Raymond said. "Maybe build it here and use driftwood, so we can save the wood near the cabin for the stove."

"I just wish I hadn't lost that meat. You're pretty lucky to have me along, you know. You wouldn't want this to be too easy."

With a grin, Raymond said, "If I ever do another raft trip, I think I'd want to have you with me. You're pretty good on those oars." He placed a big chunk of wood on the fire. "Johnny'll get another moose," he said confidently.

"Do you think Johnny wants us to stay here for the rest of the winter—if no one spots us, I mean?"

"Maybe we'll be able to hike out down the river later, on the ice, once there's no more Chinooks. I just don't know. I think we better just take our cues from Johnny from here on out."

"You won't get any back talk from me on that."

In the gray morning twilight we built up our signal fire by the river, then began moving our stuff. The squat cabin with its thick roof of moss and clay looked as miraculous as before. We broomed the dirt floor clean with spruce branches, brought our gear inside, and moved in. The stove looked to be in one piece. We fitted the stovepipe back together and ran it up through the roof jack. The big roof poles looked sound. The one window had been broken out, but a sheet of hard clear plastic had been fastened across the entire window frame. The window allowed quite a bit of light. "Home," Raymond announced. It was the twenty-first of November.

We tried a fire in the rusty little stove. It worked, and cheered us up as we warmed our hands.

I looked around the cabin, ending up with my eyes on the rough little table. "This must be the kitchen," I said.

"Needs a microwave," Raymond added. "No TV in here either. Next time we should bring a VCR—watch movies all winter."

"There you go," I said, with a small laugh that made my side hurt. But in the back of my mind, I was remembering Clint's story about the two brothers who tried to winter in Deadmen Valley, starved to death, and lost their heads to the bears.

The old man pegged the moose hide to the wall with the old nails we found around the place and began scraping the hair from the hide with the sheath knife. He was going to make it into rawhide—babiche, as Raymond called it. Raymond and I sawed three big rounds of spruce to serve as stools. We allowed our spirits to lift for the time being. All that remained of our food was a little flour, baking powder, some beans, a handful of dried fruit, and the box of meat.

Raymond and I fashioned a ladder so we'd be able to reach the food cache behind the cabin, trusting that meat would come to fill it. Like a cabin in miniature on stilts, the old cache was supported by four trees that had been sawed off about twelve feet above the ground. Just under the cache, the stilts were wrapped with stovepipe—to prevent a black bear or wolverine from reaching the cache, Raymond said.

"What about a grizzly?" I asked.

"Grizzlies can't climb," he explained. "And it's out of a grizzly's reach."

As Raymond had predicted, the old man took us out right away on a hunt for just the right birch tree. He had us cut a ten-foot log from it and carry it back to the cabin, where he planed it flat on two sides with the ax and began to strip it into lengths. "The old guys like Johnny always use birch for snowshoe frames," Raymond said. "It's tough, it'll bend without breaking, and it splits easily when it's cold."

Around noon the next day it cleared up enough for us to notice the sun making a brief appearance over the bald mountain to the southwest. The temperature was ten below, practically a heat wave. When I returned from building up the signal fire, I found Raymond watching intently as Johnny fashioned a snowshoe frame, bending the green birch strips patiently over his knee, bracing and lashing them temporarily into shape with whittled pegs and fine spruce roots. I watched for a while, until Johnny picked up his rifle, said something to us in Slavey, and slipped into the trees. He returned in the dark—no luck.

On the twenty-fifth of November the warm Chinook returned. By day it would blow through the valley almost at gale force, and by night we could hear it high above, raging on the ridges. The Nahanni opened up in spots, smoking in the cold mornings. The Chinook would alternate with the arctic winds in pitched battles that seesawed back and forth above Deadmen Valley, sending the temperature from forty above to thirty below.

Still no snow. It was not the weather that Raymond had hoped for as Johnny hunted our side of the river for the moose that should be browsing in the willow thickets. Raymond and I were picking frozen cranberries. Any we could find helped a little. We'd gone through the last of the fruit and the flour, and the ration of meat we were allowing ourselves could barely keep us going. We still had beans. For our only meal of the day, we'd been allowing ourselves no more than one pound total of the moose meat, cooked in with some beans.

When the old man wasn't hunting, he was weaving the intricate babiche lacing to complete the first pair of snowshoes. Raymond and I were making snares, braiding the thin strips of babiche as Johnny had shown us. We set a dozen snares up and down the river for snowshoe hares. Raymond knew exactly how to do it, having snared the rabbits with picture wire when he was a kid. He'd bend a young tree down over a rabbit run and rig the snare below it so it made a circle about four inches across, about three inches above the trail. Then he'd arrange slender sticks like a fence on both sides of the snare and tiny ones underneath, so the rabbit was forced to pass through the circle.

Once we interrupted a chase in the trees above us. A dark-furred animal the size of an overgrown house cat hunched its back and growled at us as we passed below. "Marten," Raymond said. In the next tree a red squirrel chattered as the marten glowered at us, growling all the while, trying at the same time to keep its eye on the squirrel. I tried to knock the marten from the tree with a stick but succeeded only in chasing it away.

Raymond was always on the lookout for fresh moose sign, but he wasn't finding any. "All these willow thickets," he kept saying. "All these moose paths. Old droppings everywhere, but none fresh. I don't understand it."

The old man showed Raymond that the airplane cable we had salvaged could make a snare too, just like a rabbit snare, only on a bigger scale. "It's illegal," Raymond said. "But in Deadmen Valley," he added with a smile, "we might get away with it." We rigged the snare on one of the more prominent moose paths through the thickets. As Raymond secured the free end to a cottonwood tree, he said, "Man, would I like to get a moose for Johnny. That's the way it's supposed to be. The young men are supposed to bring the first and best meat to the elders."

Wherever we went we took the ax with us, for protection. "Nobody walks around in the bush without a rifle," Raymond said.

I told him, "That looks more like an ax you've got in your hand."

"Better than a kick in the knee."

"Where did you come up with that expression? My mother always used to say that."

"Old Dene saying," he replied with a smirk.

"The ax . . . it's protection from what?"

"Bull moose, cow moose with a calf, or 'keep out of its way.'"

"I thought grizzlies were supposed to be hibernating by now."

"Supposed to be," he replied.

With the ax and the bow saw we made so much firewood for our little stove it looked like we had a woodlot going. We sought out the dead trees and hauled them back in lengths to the cabin and sawed and split firewood endlessly, mixing in green spruce, which split easily in the cold. With the Chinook in retreat, perhaps for good, there was plenty of cold available. We each broke a saw blade sawing too fast. When the second one broke a few days after the first, it scared us. We'd have to baby the bow saw now that we were down to the last blade.

The mercury stayed down around twenty and thirty below at midday. It amazed me that life could go on. Yet as long as we dried our clothes out overnight, and dried our gloves and mitts and the felt liners from our boots, we were okay. Bundled up in as many layers as we were, we'd become accustomed to it.

The old man made a simple hand-held drum from a small piece of moose hide that he stretched over a birch frame. It looked something like a big tambourine. He'd tap out a simple rhythm with a small padded stick, sometimes chanting on into the night. The drum had a hypnotic effect and helped take our minds from our hunger. Just as we never spoke about the search plane that didn't come back, we never talked about our hunger. It clawed at us from the inside, a private torment.

At least it was warm in the cabin. That small a space was

easy to heat if we just kept stoking the fire. After we would regretfully snuff out the candle for the evening, we'd lie on the spruce boughs in our bags and watch the bit of firelight from the stove door playing on the drumskin and the ancient face of the drummer. Each evening old Johnny started with a Slavey formula that Raymond knew and translated as "In the Distant Time it is said . . ." Raymond explained that Johnny was telling the stories "of when the world was young."

"What are they about?" I asked.

"Oh, like about Raven, how he made the world and then unmade it so it wasn't perfect anymore, how he made mosquitoes and made water to run downhill, how he'd play tricks on everybody. There's even a story about the flood like the one in the Bible. There's stories about animals back when they were human, stories about giants and supernatural beings, about heroes, about medicine men who could communicate with ravens and even take the shape of ravens . . . The elders have all sorts of stories."

All the time Johnny kept building the snowshoes. My eyes kept going back to the finished pair standing in the corner. They were truly works of art with their graceful curves and intricate rawhide webbing.

On the fifth of December it snowed six inches of dry snow, then cleared off. The sun appeared over the bald mountain only ten minutes before it set again. Raymond and I kept felling trees in the twilight, hauling logs to the cabin, splitting wood, and checking our snares. Over the next week we caught three hares, white as snow and always frozen solid by the time we discovered them. We had to bring the rabbits inside the cabin to warm them up enough to gut and skin them. Some years, Raymond said, the rabbits were everywhere you looked. There was even a legend about hares falling out of the sky like snow.

"Looks like we might have to live on rabbits," I said to Raymond. "The moose meat and beans aren't going to last much longer."

"There's no fat on rabbits," he replied. "We're going to need to find something with some fat on it. They always say your body needs to burn fat when it gets real cold."

I could see his face growing thinner, and I knew mine must be, too. I guessed I'd already lost fifteen pounds. The last of our moose meat was soon gone.

I was lucky enough to get a grouse with a well-thrown stick. It was a tasty little morsel, but it didn't take the edge off our hunger. Still no fresh sign of moose, and we hadn't heard wolves since we first arrived. Raymond was worried about not hearing the wolves anymore, and I asked him why. "No wolves means no moose," he said. "The wolves follow the moose in the winter, hoping they can get one in deep snow."

On the morning of the sixteenth of December we opened the cabin door and found Deadmen Valley transformed. Two feet of snow had fallen in the night. All the forest was draped with snow and the high mountains all around had taken on the unreality of a painting. It was all so beautiful and so *clean*, the pure whiteness of it all.

Johnny walked over to the snowshoes in the corner. To my surprise, he was motioning to me. He wanted me to try them out. "Good deal!" I said to Raymond, and we all pulled on some clothes. Outside, Johnny helped me step into them and lace up the bindings, and then I took off like a horse out of the starting gate, I guess. I hadn't gone fifteen feet before I tripped and did a faceplant in the snow. I thrashed around, spitting snow out of my mouth and trying to get back up. But I was getting all entangled, making a spectacle of myself with my arms and legs and those five-foot snowshoes all wind-milling around. Raymond and Johnny were laughing their heads off. "Hey, I thought this would be easy!" I called.

As soon as he could quit laughing, Raymond said, "Got to keep your tips up, Gabe, or they get caught in the snow. I think you better let Johnny use those now. It's a good day for him to track moose."

Johnny was still chuckling ten minutes later when he stepped into the snowshoes and laced them on. Raymond handed him the rifle and said, "Good luck, Johnny." Just then we heard wings thrashing the cold air and looked up to see a raven directly above, calling, "*Ggaagga . . . ggaagga.*"

Raymond whispered, "It's saying, 'Animal . . . animal.'" It struck me that Raymond said this as a matter of fact. He went on to whisper that ravens were known to lead hunters to game, knowing that they would get their share from what the hunter couldn't use.

The old hunter was watching as the raven tucked its wing and rolled over in the sky before flying on. Johnny winked at Raymond and nodded with a smile. "My father says it's a good-luck sign when a raven does that," Raymond explained. "It means the hunter will have good luck that day."

An hour later we heard the rifle shot loud and clear, up-river, in the cold dry air. "Moose in the cooking pot," I said, certain as if I'd seen it fall. We waited as the hours passed, and then, when Johnny hadn't returned by two we had misgivings and started after him, post-holing our way through the new snow without snowshoes.

We found where the trail of the man first intersected the trail of the moose, fresh with droppings and urine, and then we followed the trail of the man, which looped away from the moose's trail and then came back to it every quarter mile or so. "Johnny was staying downwind," Raymond explained.

We found the rifle cartridge in the snow showing where the old man had stood when he'd fired the shot. As the twi-

light deepened, we found the place where the moose had
bolted and run. No blood in the snow, not a fleck. "I guess
Johnny missed," Raymond said. His words hung in the cold air
like death.

A raven in a nearby tree caught our attention as it walked
back and forth on a dead branch, squawking and squawking.
"His belly's empty," Raymond said. "He was counting on a
moose dinner tonight. Gabe, I think I better get back to the
cabin. My boots got a little wet."

"So did mine," I told him. "We better get back fast."

Johnny was sitting by the stove in his bare feet. He
glanced up at us coming in. We were throwing off our boots
and our socks. I massaged my toes with my fingers. "They're
okay," I told Raymond, and he said, "Mine too."

We could see in the old man's mournful eyes that he'd
never caught up with the moose. He looked at Raymond and
said something in Slavey.

"No medicine," Raymond told me.

I wondered if they were talking about some medicine that
had been prescribed back in the hospital. "Let's look in the
first-aid kit," I said.

"Dene medicine," Raymond explained. "It's like power and
good luck. Different people have medicine for all sorts of
things. Hunters have good medicine for different animals.
Johnny thinks his medicine for moose is all gone. It's because
of how he left the moose above the falls. When you don't
treat an animal respectfully, its spirit is offended, and then
you won't have any more medicine with that animal. That's
what happened."

"Do you think that could be true? Do you believe it yourself?"

"I don't know," Raymond said. "I've heard that kind of
stuff all my life. It's not very scientific, I know. I guess I don't

know what I think about it."

"But at least we know there's still moose in Deadmen Valley. And he has two shells left."

"That could've been the last moose," Raymond said. To me, it sounded like he was just as convinced as the old man that we'd destroyed our luck.

■ ■ ■

"What silly ideas you have, Gramps!" This comment comes from a folk tale from India, and it's said by a flock of geese! What connections do you see between this story and The Cay?

The Clever Gander
retold by Asha Upadhyay

Once upon a time there was a flock of geese. These geese had found a home in the branches of a big banyan tree in the great Indian jungle. And every one of these geese was nothing but a silly, silly goose— except for the oldest one, who was a tough and clever old gander named Babaji, or Grandfather.

One day, Babaji noticed that a small vine was beginning to wrap itself around the banyan tree. At once he called a meeting of all the geese in the flock and told them, "See how this vine is growing up around our tree? We must destroy the vine right away while it is still weak enough for us to cut with our beaks."

But the other geese would not listen to him. "What silly ideas you have, Gramps!" they said. "How could that little vine possibly harm us?"

"It is only a tiny vine now, that is true," said Babaji. "But if we allow it to keep growing, it will soon be as strong and as high as a ladder. Then some bad person may use it to climb our tree and catch us."

"We can always find a new tree when this one is no longer safe," replied the silly geese. "There is plenty of time to worry about that."

The vine grew, stronger and stronger, taller and taller, around the banyan tree. But the silly geese paid no attention. They ignored all of Babaji's warnings and spent their days in wild goose chases.

Then one day a hunter passed by, just as the whole flock was leaving the tree to search for food. The hunter hid himself carefully behind some bushes until the geese had flown away.

"Ah-ha!" chuckled the hunter. "How lucky for me! These silly geese have kept a ladder for me to use in reaching their nests!" And he climbed easily up the vine. Working quickly, he set a trap among the nests. Then he climbed down the vine again and went home to his village.

The geese returned to the banyan tree just as it was getting dark. They did not see the trap, and before they knew it, each and every goose was snared.

The geese were terrified. They struggled to get out of the trap, but they were caught fast. Only Babaji remained calm. "You would not listen to me, you silly geese," he said. "Now we are all caught and will surely be sold in the bazaar tomorrow. It is the end of us."

The other geese became even more frightened. "Oh, Sir!" they cried. "Respected Grandfather! Please tell us how we can escape. We will do everything you tell us to do, if only you will help us out of here!"

The old gander looked at them. "Do you promise that you will listen to my advice from now on?"

The geese all promised, so the old gander told them his plan. "When the hunter returns, we will all pretend to be dead," he began. The other geese crowded around him as he explained the rest of his plan.

The next day, when the hunter came back, he saw that the geese were lying limp and lifeless in the trap. "Ah-ha!" chuckled the hunter. "How lucky for me! These silly geese were all frightened to death by being caught in my trap. That is good! Now I can carry them more easily to the market!"

And climbing up the vine, he cut each goose free from the

trap and threw them, one by one, to the ground.

The geese remained quiet, as if they really were dead, until the hunter had thrown down the last goose of the flock. Then, as the hunter began to climb back down the vine, clever old Babaji gave the signal. At that, all the geese flapped their wings and flew for their lives. They were all safely away by the time the angry hunter reached the foot of the tree.

The hunter stayed near the tree for several days, hoping that the geese would be silly enough to return to their home. And they might have been silly enough to do just that, if Babaji had not given them some better advice. He chose a new tree for them, a tree without any vines or low branches to climb on.

The geese made old Babaji their teacher and advisor, and they have learned at last not to be quite such silly geese.

■ ■ ■

Prejudice—*it does ugly things to people. In* The Cay, *Timothy knows what it's like to face prejudices and so does the writer of this story. As you read this true story from her childhood, look for the character who reminds you most of yourself. What does your choice tell you about your own attitudes?*

One More Lesson

from Silent Dancing

Judith Ortiz Cofer

I was escorted each day to school by my nervous mother. It was a long walk in the cooling air of fall in Paterson and we had to pass by El Building, where the children poured out of the front door of the dilapidated tenement, still answering their mothers in a mixture of Spanish and English: "Sí, Mami, I'll come straight home from school." At the corner we were halted by the crossing guard, a strict woman who only gestured her instructions, never spoke directly to the children, and only ordered us to "halt" or "cross" while holding her white-gloved hand up at face level or swinging her arm sharply across her chest if the light was green.

The school building was not a welcoming sight for someone used to the bright colors and airiness of tropical architecture. The building looked functional. It could have been a prison, an asylum, or just what it was: an urban school for the children of immigrants, built to withstand waves of change, generation by generation. Its red-brick sides rose to four solid stories. The black steel fire escapes snaked up its back like exposed vertebrae. A chain-link fence surrounded its concrete playground. Members of the elite safety patrol, older kids, sixth-graders mainly, stood at each of its entrances, wearing their fluorescent white belts that crisscrossed their chests and their metal badges. No one was allowed in the building until the bell rang, not even on rainy or bitter-cold days. Only the safety patrol stayed warm.

My mother stood in front of the main entrance with me and a growing crowd of noisy children. She looked like one of us, being no taller than the sixth-grade girls. She held my hand so tightly that my fingers cramped. When the bell rang, she walked me into the building and kissed my cheek. Apparently my father had done all the paperwork for my enrollment, because the next thing I remember was being led to my third-grade classroom by a black girl who had emerged from the principal's office.

Though I had learned some English at home during my first years in Paterson, I had let it recede deep into my memory while learning Spanish in Puerto Rico. Once again I was the child in the cloud of silence, the one who had to be spoken to in sign language as if she were a deaf-mute. Some of the children even raised their voices when they spoke to me, as if I had trouble hearing. Since it was a large, troublesome class composed mainly of black and Puerto Rican children, with a few working-class Italian children interspersed, the teacher paid little attention to me. I relearned the language quickly by the immersion method.

I remember one day, soon after I joined the rowdy class, when our regular teacher was absent and Mrs. D., the sixth-grade teacher from across the hall, attempted to monitor both classes. She scribbled something on the chalkboard and went to her own room. I felt a pressing need to use the bathroom and asked Julio, the Puerto Rican boy who sat behind me, what I had to do to be excused. He said that Mrs. D. had written on the board that we could be excused by simply writing our names under the sign. I got up from my desk and started for the front of the room when I was struck on the head hard with a book. Startled and hurt, I turned around expecting to find one of the bad boys in my class, but it was Mrs. D. I faced. I remember her angry face, her fingers on my arms pulling me back to my desk, and her voice saying incomprehensible things to me in a hissing tone. Someone finally explained to her that I was new, that I did not speak English. I also remember how suddenly her face changed from anger to anxiety. But I did not forgive her for hitting me with that hardcover spelling book. Yes, I would recognize that book even now. It was not until years later that I stopped hating that teacher for not understanding that I had been betrayed by a classmate and by my inability to read her warning on the board. I instinctively understood then that language is the only weapon a child has against the absolute power of adults.

I quickly built up my arsenal of words by becoming an insatiable reader of books.

■ ■ ■

A ripple and flash in the water—is it your imagination, or is something out to get you? Phillip and Timothy discover that the sea's creatures can be both fascinating and dangerous. What different kinds of pictures swim through your mind as you read these poems?

The Shark
John Ciardi

My dear, let me tell you about the shark.

Though his eyes are bright, his thought is dark.

He's quiet—that speaks well of him.

So does the fact that he can swim.

But though he swims without a sound,

Wherever he swims he looks around

With those two bright eyes and that one dark thought.

He has only one but he thinks it a lot.

And the thought he thinks but can never complete

Is his long dark thought of something to eat.

Most anything does. And I have to add

That when he eats his manners are bad.

He's a gulper, a ripper, a snatcher, a grabber.

Yes, his manners are drab. But his thought is drabber.

That one dark thought he can never complete

Of something—anything—somehow to eat.

Be careful where you swim, my sweet.

Barracuda
Dr. Joseph MacInnis

Silver

War-lord

Of the warm reef

Long

Lithe

Lonely

Lurking

Beneath the quicksilver quiver

Of the sea's surface

A regal rapier

Lying inert

Ready to strike

Large jaws moving

Open and shut

Trying the water

With age-white teeth

And eyeing

The retreating man-fish

With centuries-old disdain

■ ■ ■

"Even in the very blackest night, you can see your own hand," Phillip says of his blindness. "But I could not see mine." Helen Keller would understand—and then some. Keller was both blind and deaf. Through the help of teacher Anne Sullivan, however, she discovered the world around her when she was a young child. How well do you know your own world?

A Lesson

from The Story of My Life

Helen Keller

I recall many incidents of the summer of 1887 that followed my soul's sudden awakening. I did nothing but explore with my hands and learn the name of every object that I touched; and the more I handled things and learned their names and uses, the more joyous and confident grew my sense of kinship with the rest of the world.

When the time of daisies and buttercups came Miss Sullivan took me by the hand across the fields, where men were preparing the earth for the seed, to the banks of the Tennessee River, and there, sitting on the warm grass, I had my first lessons in the beneficence of nature. I learned how the sun and the rain make to grow out of the ground every tree that is pleasant to the sight and good for food, how birds build their nests and live and thrive from land to land, how the squirrel, the deer, the lion and every other creature finds food and shelter. As my knowledge of things grew I felt more and more the delight of the world I was in. Long before I learned to do a sum in arithmetic or describe the shape of the earth, Miss Sullivan had taught me to find beauty in the fragrant woods, in every blade of grass, and in the curves and dimples of my baby sister's hand. She linked my earliest thoughts with nature, and made me feel that "birds and flowers and I were happy peers."

But about this time I had an experience which taught me that nature is not always kind. One day my teacher and I were returning from a long ramble. The morning had been fine, but it was growing warm and sultry when at last we turned our faces homeward. Two or three times we stopped to rest under a tree by the wayside. Our last halt was under a wild cherry tree a short distance from the house. The shade was grateful, and the tree was so easy to climb that with my teacher's assistance I was able to scramble to a seat in the branches. It was so cool up in the tree that Miss Sullivan proposed that we have our luncheon there. I promised to keep still while she went to the house to fetch it.

Suddenly a change passed over the tree. All the sun's warmth left the air. I knew the sky was black, because all the heat, which meant light to me, had died out of the atmosphere. A strange odour came up from the earth. I knew it, it was the odour that always precedes a thunderstorm, and a nameless fear clutched at my heart. I felt absolutely alone, cut off from my friends and the firm earth. The immense, the unknown, enfolded me. I remained still and expectant; a chilling terror crept over me. I longed for my teacher's return; but above all things I wanted to get down from that tree.

There was a moment of sinister silence, then a multitudinous stirring of the leaves. A shiver ran through the tree, and the wind sent forth a blast that would have knocked me off had I not clung to the branch with might and main. The tree swayed and strained. The small twigs snapped and fell about me in showers. A wild impulse to jump seized me, but terror held me fast. I crouched down in the fork of the tree. The branches lashed about me. I felt the intermittent jarring that came now and then, as if something heavy had fallen and the shock had traveled up till it reached the limb I sat on. It worked my suspense up to the highest point, and just as I was thinking the tree and I should fall together, my teacher seized my hand and helped me down. I clung to her, trembling with joy to feel the earth under my feet once more. I had learned a new lesson—that nature "wages open war against her children and under softest touch hides treacherous claws."

■ ■ ■

Theodore Taylor

■ (born 1921) ■

Believing that personal experience is a writer's richest resource, Theodore Taylor has held an amazing variety of jobs. He has been a merchant sailor and a naval officer; the manager of a prize fighter; a reporter and a magazine writer; and a movie publicist, producer, screenwriter, and documentary filmmaker. These careers have taken him all over the world.

Although he showed a sense of adventure early on, little else in Taylor's early life suggested his future careers. The youngest of Edward and Elnora Taylor's six children, Theodore came into the world on July 23, 1921. Life never was easy for the family. During the Great Depression, Taylor's father was gone for months at a time, seeking work in steel mills. Even as a child, Taylor helped support the family by selling candy, picking up scrap metal to sell at the junkyard, and delivering newspapers. "It did not occur to me until years later," he noted in an interview, "that there was anything exceptional about a boy just shy of ten getting up at four-thirty to walk to a local hotel, pick up sixty-odd newspapers, deliver them by seven, come home, have breakfast and go off to school."

Despite hard times, Taylor remembers his childhood in rural North Carolina as "one short happy adventure." An extremely independent child, Taylor enjoyed roaming by himself through muddy fields, fishing docks, and old brickyards.

Taylor began his career as a professional writer when he was only thirteen years old, writing a sports column for the Portsmouth (Virginia) *Evening Star*. His pay was just fifty cents a week, but he learned much from the experience. Four years later, Taylor joined the Washington *Daily News* as a copy boy. There, he learned to write simply and directly. By the age of nineteen, he was an NBC network sportswriter.

When World War II broke out, Taylor joined the United States Merchant Marine and the Naval Reserve. He served aboard a gasoline tanker in the Atlantic and the Pacific; then, the navy called him up as a cargo officer. Taylor's wartime experiences later helped him as he wrote his first book, *The Magnificent Mitscher* (published in 1954).

Hollywood became Taylor's home after the war. Work as a press agent led him into filmmaking—first as a story editor and then as an associate producer of documentary films. At the same time, Taylor's writing career blossomed. His second book was *Fire on the Beaches* (published in 1958), about the impact of German submarines during World War II. While doing research for that book, Taylor came across an account of the sinking of a small Dutch ship. An eleven-year-old boy survived the sinking but eventually was lost at sea, alone on a life raft. That incident gave Taylor the idea for *The Cay*.

Taylor used his Hollywood experiences to write his first book for younger readers, *People Who Make Movies* (published in 1967). The positive response to the book astonished him; in fact, more than three thousand students wrote to him, commenting upon the book and asking for advice about Hollywood careers. Inspired, Taylor tried a novel—and the result was *The Cay* (published in 1969). More books for young readers have followed, including *The Children's War, Teetoncey, The Odyssey of Ben O'Neal, The Trouble with Tuck, The Hostage, Sweet Friday Island, Sniper, The Weirdo, Timothy of the Cay* (a "prequel-sequel" to *The Cay*), and *The Bomb*.

Taylor and his wife Flora live in Laguna Beach, California. Highly disciplined, Taylor writes from 8:30 a.m. until 4:30 or 5:00 p.m., seven days a week—except during football season, when he takes weekends off to root for his favorite teams.